Press One for Murder

By Peter Tompkins

CONTENTS

Disclaimer:

This is a book of fiction. No one was hurt, injured or murdered during before or after its inception. The bank and all of the characters within this book are fictional. No banking customers were hurt or murdered during before or after this books inception.

1 PREFACE

Why did I write Press One for Murder?

I am what I refer to as a "Call Center Survivor". That is a person who has worked in a corporate call center and lived to tell about it.

You might say, "A survivor? Come on Pete! How hard could it possibly be to work in a call center taking calls from customers all day?" Trust me, it's one of the hardest jobs in the world with the least amount of rewards.

I have worked in various and sundried corporate call centers since 1990. I have been the annoying telemarketer calling you on the phone to sell you a magazine subscription or a credit card. I have also been the customer service representative who listened to your long unfathomable story behind why you overdrew your bank account and how you should not be charged overdraft fees because your dog just died. While not all of the places I worked were, "modern day sweat shops", I can easily say that ninety percent of them were. So, that leaves ten percent that were at least tolerable. Not a very good ratio.

There are call centers in India, so stressful that they have jumping nets surrounding the perimeter of the building roofs to keep employees from jumping to their deaths. People who have worked in these call centers and lived to tell about it are definitely, "Call Center Survivors".

While my book is a fictional murder mystery I can tell you that I personally have never harmed or murdered anyone. No one was harmed during the writing of this book or before it was written. That being said, this story stems from a conversation I had with an abusive customer while I was working for a major technology company many years ago. My customer demanded credits to his account that he was not entitled to. After attempting to follow protocol by offering him a small dollar amount as a credit he threated to come to our call center and do myself and my co-workers bodily harm.

1

After his thinly veiled threat he proceeded to read to me our call centers address and where each of us entered and exited the building. I responded by asking him if he thought it was wise to threaten me and my company when before my very eyes on my computer screen I had his name, social security number, address, where he worked and all his spouses corresponding information. He promptly hung up. I notified security.

The next day we had two police cars parked in front of our building. They remained stationed at our front door twenty-four hours a day seven days a week for the next two months. One can only assume they were there due to my conversation with one of our customers.

My conversation with the abusive "gentleman" from that day sent me into a deep day dream about writing a book about a call center representative that hates his job and his customers. Some of his customers turn up dead. How they died, I'll leave it to you to find out by reading the following chapters.

Sweat shops of the nineteenth and early twentieth centuries.

During the late eighteen-hundreds, the clothing industry employed men, woman and children in their factories as manual laborers. Many of these workplaces attracted immigrants, the rural poor and those who were desperate for work. They worked for extremely low wages, long hours extremely poor conditions and many health risks. Many of these establishments were over crowded, poorly ventilated, and prone to fires and rat infestations. Because of the horrendous working environment, they became known as sweat shops.

Here in the United States, labor unions and labor laws slowly did away with textile sweat shops over time. Much of the clothing industry that was once housed here in the U.S., has been off-shored to Taiwan, Vietnam and China.

The Modern Day Sweat Shop

Fortunately, the days of poorly ventilated, rat infested factories have gone by the wayside. Unfortunately, the days sweat shops have not. You and I speak to people who work in modern day sweat shops every time we pick up the phone and dial the toll-free number that connects us with the customer service department of the corporate offices of our bank, cable company or any number of services that we have brought into our lives.

The modern day sweat shop is the corporate call center. Why do I say this you ask? You may even say, *"There is no way the working conditions are anywhere near as bad as the textile factories of the early industrial age."* Perhaps not. At least not literally. Let's just say that corporations have ways of skirting the laws to make the call center working environment appear to be safe and legal.

The call center itself is usually a larger rectangular room ranging in size anywhere from ten thousand to one million square feet. While they are not prone to rat infestation or fires they still can be toxic work environments. Often-times they are housed in a section of the corporate headquarters that is windowless, poorly lit and usually poorly ventilated.

They employ anywhere from several hundred to several thousand employees of all ages and walks of life. All are forced to sit for up to five hours at a time in cramped four foot by three-foot cubicles without being allowed to leave their work station for food, water or a bathroom break.
Since unions are quickly becoming a thing of the past, most call centers are not unionized. The ones that are don't seem to be any better than the centers that are not.

Most of the toxicity within a call center stems from emotional and mental duress. After a brief two-week training period where employees must learn the company's entire portfolio of products and learn to navigate anywhere from ten to twenty computer systems, they are immediately given a headset, given a desk and start taking calls. They are immediately required to meet and maintain certain metrics that measure their performance while taking inbound calls from customers. Many if not all required metrics are impossible to meet right away. Over time? Yes. But within six months? No.

In traditional inbound call centers, each customer service representative must receive the call, determine the customers concern, resolve their concern and sell the customer a product that they determine would be beneficial in a polite and professional manner within seven minutes. This "seven minutes" is known in the call center industry as "handle time" or "talk time". If a customer services reps handle time averages out to be longer than seven minutes within a thirty-day time frame the employee is disciplined by their supervisor. This takes place during a thirty-day performance review. First infraction for long handle time is a verbal warning from their immediate supervisor. A second infraction is a written warning. A third infraction is a final written warning and then termination. At termination, there is "the walk of shame". The employee is ceremoniously walked out of the call center in front of their peers flanked by their supervisor and the head of human resources and to the parking lot.

Toxicity also stems from the verbally abusive and belligerent customers who feel they have the right to belittle and demean the person they are speaking to. They become remarkably sadistic when they have charges on their account they don't recognize or if they can't remember the security questions they personally set up to keep unauthorized users from accessing their information. Customers will insult your race, heritage, sex and anything else that comes to their minds when they desperately seek something that they know they don't deserve. If a customer service representative shows even the slightest signs of weakness, that's when the customers smells blood and goes in for the "kill". Not even your mother is spared by the verbal assault you must endure in their attempt to get you to submit to their will. In modern day call-center you are not permitted to hang up on a customer regardless how abusive they become.

It's a very sedentary position. You are not permitted to move from your desk. Most corporate call centers require their employees to take calls from the corporations, customer base for up to four hours at a time with only a ten-minute break. If an employee leaves their desk for any reason outside of their allotted ten-minute break they are immediately punished. As mentioned in the previous paragraph for handle time infractions, first infraction for leaving their work station is a verbal warning from their immediate supervisor. A second infraction is a written warning. A third infraction is a final written warning then termination.

The extraordinary pressure placed on the employee to improve their performance is compounded by getting little to no additional assistance or guidance on how to improve from their supervisor. It's literally left up to the employee to figure it out for themselves. With only two ten-minute breaks and a half hour lunch for free time they are forced to make-adjustments to their performance while receiving calls from customers on the phones. It's a "baptism by fire", "sink or swim" mentality that leads to the industry slogan, "Fake it till you make it."

Food nor drink is permitted at their desks. To decrease the risk of a customer's sensitive financial information from being stolen, personal items such as wallets, coats, purses nor cell phones are permitted on the call center floor at any employees work stations. Any infraction leads to additional disciplinary action.

The majority of supervisors, who oversee the staff are promoted from the ranks. Many get promoted after only being on the job for six months. Most have no management experience. This is a perfect recipe for disaster. Inexperienced, poorly trained customer service reps being supervised by managers who have only been on the job for six months with no management experience adds to the sweat shop asylum atmosphere. This compounds the frustration and pressure that employees experience.

All of These ingredients combined, create a tremendous amount of turnover. Many of the call centers where I have been employed start with a training class of thirty new employees. Six months after graduating from training there are typically six employees remaining from the original class. That's a turnover of eighty percent. Many will leave the company due to attendance issues which are more-often than not, brought on by employees not wanting to come into work so, they call in sick. Others leave for performance issues such as not meeting the metrics. While others succumb to the pressure of the job and simply do not return to work. One day they make up their mind that they just can't take it anymore. I have seen employees take off their headsets in the middle of their shift, set the headset down on their desk and walk out the door never to return.

Several call centers where I have been employed had weekly visits from the paramedics. One day I heard a loud thump and felt the floor shake. I looked across the aisle and one of my female co-workers had hit the deck and was lying unconscious on the floor. After 911 was called the paramedics arrived. They rolled their gurney onto the call center floor and removed the lady who collapsed. She and others like her never returned to work.

The following story is dedicated to all the people who are currently employed in call centers and all the call center survivors. Each of us have our own experience. Some experiences good but most of them are very bad. Some employees find a great deal of success working in a call center but their stories are few and far between.

This book is also for all the current and former call center employees from around the world who I have spoken to through my YouTube channel, http://www.youtube.com/ptpop. We all share similar call center experiences. I have conversed with some wonderful people from the United States, United Kingdom, The Philippines, Canada, Australia, India, Dominican Republic, Costa Rica, Mexico, Germany, France and many others. Without your support my channel would not exist. Before I started publishing my videos about working in call centers I thought I was alone in my perspective on call centers. Each of you helped me realize I was not alone.
Thank you.

2 the first victim

A clap of thunder and a flash of lightning shattered the still of the night as Ms. Shanower settled in behind the wheel of her silver Ford F-150 while driving west on Memorial Parkway. In the bed of her truck sat ten black trash bags filled with garbage. A cold freezing November rain spattered against her windshield as she lit a cigarette with her lighter. After rolling the driver's side window down half way she blew a pale blue plume of smoke out of the corner of her mouth through the opened window and into the night air.

Tonight, she was on her Friday night mission. She had been on a tight budget since her husband passed away the previous year. Any way she could find a way to cut corners was her top priority. The city of Akron had been charging her $45 a month to pick up her trash and she was not about to use or pay for the service. Instead of walking her trash to the curb at the end of her driveway she would take her garbage to a local apartment complex and deposit it in their dumpster.

Every Friday night she would gather her garbage bags and toss them into the back of her truck and drive them over to The Maple House Apartments on the edge of town. She despised The Maple House Apartments because they housed low income and section eight families that she felt were the cause for the decline of her neighborhood.

As she drove through the night rain, her disgust for these people intensified. Her mouth twisted into a grimace as her mind filled with distorted visions of the welfare dependent single mothers, drug addicts, prostitutes and gang bangers that infested the grounds of those apartments. She wished someone would burn it to the ground.

She thought to herself,
"Trashy people can always use some more trash. So, that's what I'll give them."

Her truck slowly crawled into the driveway of the apartments. Navigating the parking lot cratered with pot holes from the previous winter, she drove to the back of the apartment complex. It was an L shaped, three-story brown brick building that was built in the early 1960's. In that era, it was considered to be "modern apartment living". Over the years, it had changed hands several times. The current management company was a well-known slum lord run by Nick Pappalardo. He seemed to have a knack for letting properties decline.

She pulled up along-side the dumpster located at the back of the parking lot. It was pushed up against an old chain link fence with razor wire at the top. She loved its location. Hidden in the shadows and just out of reach of the glow of the solitary street light perched above the parking lot no one could see her when she arrived to deposit her trash. It was Inconspicuously hidden behind the end of north wing of the building where none of the residents had windows or balconies.

Teeming with trash, it looked as if it had vomited shiny black trash bags, beer cans, fast food wrappers, pizza boxes, pallets and used tampon applicators onto the asphalt. An old torn and stained mattress laying on its side was leaning propped up against the front. Scattered on the pavement beside the dumpster and in front of the chain link fence were discarded hypodermic needles.

Ms. Shanower pulled in front of the dumpster and put her truck in park. After quickly surveying the parking lot for vagrants she cautiously opened her door and stepped out. Stepping towards the bed of her truck something squished beneath her left foot. As she lifted her foot to observe what made the sound, the yellow glow from the dome light of her truck revealed a used condom stuck to the sole of her shoe.

She choked back vomit and covered her mouth with her right hand as she scraped the condom from her shoe by dragging it across the pavement.

In disgust she exclaimed,

"Dirty filthy white trash fuckers. I am surprised they even have the presence of mind to use contraception."

Rain spattered on the ground as she reached into the bed of the truck and hoisted out two of the garbage bags, turned and then tossed them onto the pavement in front of the dumpster. As she turned to grasp two more bags she froze when she heard what sounded like a man groaning. It sounded like he was behind the dumpster.

"Probably some junkie passed out from an over dose." She said to herself in disgust under hear breath.

After grabbing two more trash bags from the bed of her truck she started to toss them when from the shadows behind the dumpster a man called out her name,

"Ms. Shanower?"

She dropped both bags onto the pavement and stared in the direction where she thought the voice came. Her voice trembled as she asked,

"Who is that? How do you know my name?"

"Ms. Shanower, I am so disappointed with you. Are the garbage men on strike in your neighborhood?"

Her body began to shake. Turning to her right she attempted to get back into her truck but she tripped over one of the garbage bags that she had just dropped and fell to the ground. Her forehead banged off the edge of the door splitting it wide opened. Blood streamed into her eyes and down her face. She struggled to a sitting position and attempted to scream but could only make a tortured choking sound.

The man in the shadows said,

"Ms. Shanower. I am sorry. It's time for me to take the trash out."

The assailant raised a nickel plated .Smith and Wesson 357 with his right arm and fired. A solitary bright flash of light and a loud bang echoed off the walls of the apartments. The back of Ms. Shanower's head exploded spraying pieces of skull fragments and brain matter onto the back-quarter-panel of her truck. Her lifeless body slumped sideways draping itself limply over the bag of trash that she had just stumbled over.

Her attacker stepped from the shadows. In his left, he held a plain white business card. One side of the card had a message printed on it that read, "Press One for Murder. "Looking down at Ms. Shanower, he tossed the card towards her. It fluttered to the ground and landed in the growing pool of blood behind her head on the ground.

He quietly walked into the shadows, and disappeared.

A small stream of rain diluted blood ran across the pavement, through a sewer grate and into the storm sewer fifteen feet from her now lifeless body.

3 the crime scene

As far back as Captain David Tarmelli could remember he wanted to be a police officer. After joining the force in 1981 he walked the beat in the fourth precinct for several years and then moved to the street crime unit. After working the street crime unit, he was promoted to detective in homicide.

It was 2:30pm and he finally found time to break away from a mountain of paperwork to eat his lunch. From a blue plastic grocery bag, he pulled cold Swiss and ham salad sandwich on rye, potato chips and a can of Classic Coke. Aside from the occasional bag of Beef Jerky purchased from the vending machine, this had been the backbone of his nutrition for more than thirty years.

For the first time this week he was actually going to have a chance to eat his lunch.
He picked up his sandwich with both hands, closed his eyes and took a large bite. Ham salad oozed from the two pieces of rye bread and dripped from his mouth and onto his wrinkled white button-down dress shirt. As he wiped his mouth with his shirt sleeve, the phone rang.

"God damn it! Just once let me eat my God damn lunch in peace." He shouted as he answered his phone.

"4th Precinct. Tarmelli. This better be good. You're interrupting a delicious ham salad sandwich."

10

"Tom. It's Sergeant Jamerson with the Street Crime Unit. I am at a new crime scene. We got one victim with a single gunshot to the head behind the Maple House Apartments.

"Any sign of a struggle?"

Sergeant Jamerson cleared his voice and replied,

"Well, her forehead was cracked open. It's a pretty sizable gash. We'll have to see what CSI says but I don't know what would have split her head open. We found a business card laying on the ground near her. There is a hand-written message on the card that reads, "Press One for Murder"."

Tarmelli exclaimed,

"Press one for murder? What the hell does that mean?

"Not sure Captain. It was lying in a pool of the victim's blood. We bagged it as evidence. It looks like this murderer may be leaving his calling card."

"Sounds like it."

"What does the scene look like at this time?"

"Well, we have a single victim. Her I.D. says she's Ms. Gloria Shanower. She's 45-year-old white female, shot once in the head. The crime scene is behind the apartment building in front of the dumpster. She's lying next to her truck. The engine is running. Her purse is sitting on the passenger seat with all of her credit cards, I.D., fifty dollars and some change inside. So, it wasn't a car-jacking or a robbery. The business card was lying in a pool of blood next to the victim's head."

"Are there any other victims? Any witnesses?"

"No other victims. We've been knocking on resident's doors but no one saw anything. The only security cameras cover the doors and the parking lot. Nothing points toward the crime scene."

"Let's see if the management office will let us take a look at the camera footage from those cameras. You never know what they saw.

"Sounds good. Tom. I'll get them working on it now."

Ok. I'll be down there in 15 minutes. Makes sure the Crime Scene Unit bags everything."

"Sounds good Tom.

Captain Tarmelli sat back in his chair for a moment and stared at his sandwich and said,

"Well little buddy, you want to go for a ride? I am afraid we've got to eat and run."

He gathered up his sandwich, chips and Coke from his desk and hastily slid it back into the grocery bag. He grabbed his Glock 17 from his top right desk drawer and slid it into his shoulder holster? After putting on his brown tweed sports jacket he walked out of the room, to the parking garage and got into his car.

The twenty-minute drive to The Maple Apartments was just long enough for Tarmelli to enjoy his sandwich and potato chips. He let out a large putrid belch as he pulled into the parking lot of the apartments and put his Chevy Suburban into park. After wiping ham salad from his chin, he stepped from his vehicle where he was immediately greeted by Sergeant Jamerson.

Sergeant Jamerson greeted Captain Tarmelli,
"Hey there chief. We have a lady that lives here that says she has seen this victim around here every Friday night. But she didn't see the shooting."

"Let's go talk to her."

Jamerson and Tarmelli walked behind the building and to the crime scene. Standing on the edge of the crime scene tape was an emaciated white, middle age woman with brown dreadlocks wearing a southwestern serape, ripped pajama bottoms and a black boulder derby.

As they approached Jamerson said,

"Ms. Haddlemock? This is Captain Tarmelli. He would like to ask you a few questions if you don't mind."

Ms. Haddlemock, shivering from standing in the rain, replied,

"Sure. I aint in no trouble am I officer?"

Captain Tarmelli responded as he reached out to shake her hand,

"No ma'am. Why would you think you're in trouble dear?"

"Well, I have been having some problems getting off the stuff."

"The stuff? You mean you're an addict ma'am?"

"Well, I don't want to get put in prison for shooting up or nothing."

"Ma'am. I am sorry to hear that you have some issues with drug addiction but I am here to talk with you about a murder. I can assure you I am not going to run you downtown over anything to do with your drug habit. What can you tell me about what you saw?"

"Officer, I didn't see the murder but I have seen the lady who got herself shot by the dumpster. She's comes around here every Friday night."

"Do you buy drugs from her?"

"Oh dear no. She comes in to the parking lot every night and throws her trash in our dumpster. She gets back in her truck and leaves."

"Do you live here ma'am?"

"Yeah. I got a place here with my sister Ethel. We shoot-up by the dumpster sometimes. Especially on Friday nights. That's where her dealer, Little Man, meets us."
"Have you ever seen her fighting or arguing with anyone? Does she talk to you?"

"No. I never saw her with anyone. She comes in here by herself. She saw me and Ethel one night and called us filthy white trash whores and sped out of here with her tires burning rubber. But that's it."

"Where were you tonight?"

"Little Man didn't show up tonight. We stood out there for a good hour but he never showed. So, we went back inside and watched Jeopardy on the T.V."

"Can anyone verify that?"

"Sure can. The superintendent had to let us in the building and our apartment because we locked ourselves out."

"Did you see anyone that looked out of place tonight. Any unusual activity?"

"Nope. Nothing. Just Little Man not showing up. That's it."

"What is Little Man's real name?"

"I have no idea officer. We just give him his money and he give us what we need."

"Ok. Ms. Haddlemock. Here's one of my cards. If you think of anything else please give me a call."

"Sure, will officer. Did someone kill this lady because she was using our dumpster?"

"We're not sure yet. Thank you for your time."

Ms. Haddlemock walked back to the apartment building and went inside. Tarmelli said to Sergeant Jamerson,

"Let's make sure they tag the bags of trash that Ms. Shanower brought here. Have them bring them in for analysis. There may be something in the trash that will give us a clue."

"Sure, thing chief."

"I wonder if Little Man is part of this."

"I was thinking the same thing. Let's take a look around the crime scene to see if there is anything that jumps out at us."

As the two officers approached the dumpster Tarmelli yelled,

"Has anyone looked inside the dumpster yet?"

An officer in a blue rain poncho yelled back,

"Not yet chief."

"Ok. Let's take a look inside."

The officer walked over to the dumpster. As he began to carefully remove two bags of trash from the top of the heap he yelled,

"Captain! Get over here! I think we have another victim.

Tarmelli and Jamerson quickly scurried beneath the crime scene tape and ran to the dumpster.
Looking inside they saw the fist of an African American man rising up from the garbage. Stuck between the index and middle finger was a plain white business card with an identical message written on it, "Press One for Murder".

In a despondent voice Tarmelli said,

"It looks like we may have a serial killer on our hands.

Sergeant Jamerson responded,

"Sure, does chief."

Tarmelli rubbed his eyes as if he were trying to wipe away everything he had just seen and said,
"Let's get our second victim out of the dumpster and see who he is. This could be Little Man. We've got a really messy crime scene but we have to sift through everything and tag everything that is relevant. Look for shell casings too.

Just as Tarmelli was finishing his instructions the Crime Scene Investigation van pulled into the parking lot. Three men and one women appeared from the van wearing navy blue windbreakers. Written on the back of each windbreaker in bright yellow block letters was the abbreviation C.S.I.

Tarmelli walked over to the van and directed the officers,

"Ok. I am Captain Tarmelli. I'm in charge of the crime scene. We've got two victims. One is on the ground in front of the dumpster and the other is inside the dumpster. Let's remove our victim from the dumpster and the contents of the dumpster so we can see what else we can find inside. Tag everything so we know where it was when you found it. Be as careful as possible. I know it's a trash can but our killer has to have left some evidence in there that will help us find him. Let's go through the bags that Ms. Shanower, the victim next to the truck, left behind and see if there are any clues in there as to who would want to see her dead. "

4 Another day

As it had a thousand mornings before, Jeremy Grant's clock radio came to life. 5:40 AM always seemed to arrive right after he closed his eyes at 11:00pm the night before. WGAM 850's morning news man, Roger Mauer, was giving the local traffic and weather report in Akron.

"Well, winter is here. While you were sleeping, a cold front moved in and it's a steamy 28 degrees outside. Along with a lot of ice on the roadways. So, we have a couple of accidents and a massive slowdown on the west bound lanes of I-90. Looks like a big rig has jack knifed on dead mans-curve. So, if you're coming in from the east side better give yourself a little extra time on the way to work."

Jeremy shivered as he rolled over and leaned on his left shoulder with one eye open and squinted through his sleep encrusted eyelid to see what time it was. He yearned to squeeze in a few more minutes of sleep before he had to get up and get ready for work. Rubbing his eyes, he focused and refocused but all he could see was red distorted blotches on the face of his digital alarm clock.

Blindly reaching for his wire rimmed glasses on the night stand he knocked over a half full wine glass of Chardonnay that was left over from the night before. The wine splashed onto the table top and into the speaker on the side of the clock radio sending sparks and smoke into the air. The clock radio went dark. Slowly swinging his legs over the side of the bed he chuckled deeply as he sarcastically said to himself,

"It looks like I really do have a drinking problem."

The noxious smell of sulfur from the smoke stacks of a nearby steel mill wafted through his bedroom window. He sat naked on the edge of the bed with his eyes closed for a few moments trying to get his aching mind to focus. His thoughts were still wading through a wine and sleeping pill induced haze.

16

There was a time when he loved to sleep. He looked at it as a way of escaping reality. Each night his dreams used to be a new adventure. They were colorful, vivid and wondrous dreamscapes that provided sanctuary from his life as a Customer Service Representative in a call center for a local bank.

There was a time in his life when he could sleep anywhere. He once slept so soundly on the floor of the airport while waiting for a flight that he missed his flight. But as he got older, sleep escaped him. He battled with insomnia. It was driving him to the brink of insanity. He turned to wine and sleeping pills to help him drift off. But his drug induced slumber turned his dreams into a twisted and horrifying landscape of demented shadowy figures leading him through a labyrinth of darkness and torment.

He hung his head and said to out loud himself,
"My God! Why can't I sleep anymore? God? Isn't my life bad enough. Do you really have to take sleep away from me too? God damn you God. Damn you! The one thing left in my life that I actually enjoyed, and you had to take that away from me too didn't you. Well, fuck you God and the horse you rode in on you old bearded archaic bastard you!"

Pulling on his glasses he pushed himself up and out of the bed. His ankles and knees popped as he slowly made his way from the bedroom down the hall and into the kitchen. Four years as the star running back at his local high school and fourteen years of heavy drinking had started to catch up to his thirty-two-year-old body.

"Coffee! I must have coffee. " He said out loud.

After plugging in the coffee pot, he opened the cupboard door above the sink where he kept a canister of Cup-O-Java coffee and removed it from the shelf and placed it on the counter. It seemed extremely light. In a panic, he hastily removed the round yellow lid to discover that the container was empty. Only a few tiny dark brown grounds scattered at bottom of the can remained.

"God damn it! No fucking coffee?"

In a blind rage, he whirled his body around and with all of his might he hurled the empty canister of coffee at his antique dark cherry wood corner cupboard in the corner of the kitchen. The canister shattered a pane of glass, bounced up into the air and dropped and rattled on the ground, bouncing twice before it came to rest at his feet.

He screamed,

"Damn it Jeremy! Can't you do anything, right? Anything? I guess mom was correct. I guess I need a keeper because I sure can't seem to take care of myself. Well fuck it. I'll get coffee once I am at work."

After eating his usual breakfast, a bowl of granola cereal, a glass of orange juice and one mutli-vitamin, he proceeded to the bathroom to relieve himself and take a shower.

He flicked the wall switch inside the bathroom door turning on the bathroom lights. Two fluorescent lights on either side of the mirror above his avocado green ceramic bathroom sink sputtered and crackled to life. As he looked in the mirror he saw a bald, middle-aged man with bags beneath his vacant eyes staring back at him. His entire body was saturated with a sickening green hue from the glow of the bluish-green fluorescent light. As he ran his hands over his protruding gut that hung over the waste-band of his Fruit of the Loom tighty whities like he a proud mother caressing her unborn child he said to himself,

"Oh God! What happened to me? Look at the bags beneath my eyes. Look at that gut."

Stepping to his left he moved and in front of his toilet he leaned forward with both arms outstretched in front of him, palms of each hand against the wall behind the toilet. He strategically placed his legs around and himself above the toilet bowl, closed his eyes, lowered his head and pushed. A reddish hue appeared on his face as he attempted to urinate. After what seemed to be an eternity a small trickle of urine dribbled from his urethra and into the toilet bowl below. As he relaxed the trickle turned into an intermittent steady stream flooding the bowl with warm yellow liquid. Reaching down with his right hand he squeezed out any remaining urine from his member and flushed.

Mindlessly pulling back the plain white moldy plastic shower curtain over the tub and stepping into the old white cast porcelain claw foot tub he thought to himself,

"One of these days, I am going to clean this place up."

His feet ached from the coldness of the porcelain beneath his feet as he turned on the cold then the hot water, adjusted it to a comfortable temperature and pulled up the stopper on the faucet to engage the shower. With eyes closed he basked in the warm water as it washed over his body. His mind was filled with what lay ahead of him at work: Eight hours a day, disembodied voices of customers screaming at him while he was leashed to his desk by a Plantronics headset. Visions of Christine, his morbidly obese supervisor, who wreaked of moth balls and insisted on flossing her teeth at her desk while she reviewed his performance with him, flashed before his eyes. The African American lady who sat to his right who obsessively cleaned her left ear every five minutes with a bobby pin made his stomach churn. It was a modern-day freak show and he was slowly becoming one of the freaks. He was slowly falling apart and wasn't sure how much longer he could endure his existence.

After washing, he returned to his bedroom and put on his corporate uniform: Tan khaki pants, blue polo shirt and comfortable brown penny loafers. His wallet slipped from his hand as he grabbed it from the top of the dresser. A sharp pain shot from his lower back and down his right leg as he bent over to pick it up. He shrieked and fell to his knees. The pain slowly subsided, he regained his composure and placed his wallet in his back-right pocket and slowly stood back up.

One of the most demoralizing things about his uniform was his picture printed on his thin plastic security badge. He had to show the badge to security every day even after he swiped it over the security sensor on the outside of the building. Every single day the security guard would smirk and say, "Nice picture dude."

The security badge was the size of a playing card and made from thin white plastic. It gave him access to the building where the call center was housed. His picture was printed in the center and it was taken on his first day of work ten years earlier. He looked high in the photograph because the security guard that took it captured him with his eyes half open. The guard refused to re-take the picture due to budget restrictions.

He clipped his security badge, which was inside a clear vinyl envelope and attached to a retractable security card holder lanyard, to the front right belt loop of his pants.

With his car keys in his right hand he walked out of his bedroom to the door of his apartment. Pausing for a moment before he turned the door knob to leave his apartment and go to work he took a deep breath. The brass knob felt cold and slimy as his sweaty hands twisted it open and walked out and to his car parked in the parking lot.

As he walked towards his car his eyes scanned the northwestern horizon. His heart sank as he observed the flannel grey winter skies of November approaching. November always brought with it an ominous cold front that would entomb northeast Ohio with ice and snow for the next six months. Winter was here to stay.

Jeremy's grey 1998 Honda Accord was entombed in a thin sheet of ice. When Jeremy went to be the night before it was a was seventy-eight degree and a warm gentle rain had begun to fall. Overnight the temperatures had dropped fifty degrees. The cold front that had moved in brought with it sub-freezing temperatures. The parking lot where Jeremy parked his car was now covered in a treacherous sheet of ice. He struggled to keep his balance has he slipped and slid on the surface of the icy parking lot on the way to his car. Under his breath he cursed,

"God, damn it! Now I am going to spend the next 15 minutes scraping the windows and I'll be late to work. God, damn it all to hell!"

After unlocking the car, he opened the driver's door. The ice creaked and crackled as the door moved outward into an open position. The sound reminded him of opening an old rust encrusted door to a mummy's tomb.

Careful of his aching back he slowly lowered himself into the driver's seat. Once inside, he placed his hands on the steering wheel for leverage to help him carefully pull each of his legs into the car and then put the key into the ignition and started the car. After turning on the heat and the rear defroster he sat back with his eyes closed, head against the head rest and thought to himself,

"Just a few more minutes of sleep."

But he couldn't. He had been late twice this month and Christine; his supervisor had been threatening to give him a written warning if he showed up late again. He didn't need to be any later than he was already going to be. A written warning meant no bonus for the month and no raise for the year.

Opening his eyes, he leaned forward and opened the glove compartment and pulled out a blue plastic ice scraper. Printed in white letters across the front of the blade to the scraper was his insurance agents company name, "Bill Bruce Life, Property & Casualty".

Jeremy pulled himself out of the car and began to scrape the windshield. The defrosters had begun to defrost the ice over the driver's side and passenger side of the windshield making it easier to scrape the ice away. Some of the ice peeled from the window like sheets of glass and fell to the pavement shattering into hundreds of little pieces. He said out loud,

"Thanks Bill Bruce, it looks like your dandy ice scraper came in handy today. At least your sorry ass is good for something other than trying to sell me life insurance."

The rear defroster had done its job by melting little horizontal slats in the rear windshield. He could see out of the front and the back. The ice on the side windows was a piece of cake. Jeremy simply walked around the car and gave each window a quick firm karate chop with the side of his hand and the ice cracked and fell to the ground.

"Well, that's not as bad as I thought. Only 10 minutes late. At least the car is warmed up."
He said out loud.

He got back inside the car, closed his door and put the car into drive and slowly pulled out of the parking lot. Turning left onto Broadview Road his mood grew dark as he anticipated the forty-minute drive that lay ahead of him. Even worse was the thought of what waited for him at the end of his drive; the grey, windowless concrete bunker that housed the modern sweat shop where he worked, Midland Bank.

The lack of windows in his building was due to the fact the it contained the banks massive main vault that supplied all the branches with cash. Armored cars ferried thousands of dollars each day to and from the branches like little honey bees flying to and from the hive. Millions of dollars were stored somewhere deep in the bowels of the building. So, windows were kept out of the original architectural design just in case there was an attack on the building by terrorists, bank robbers or in the event of an unlikely nuclear strike.
Armed guards prowled the grounds on foot and on golf carts. Razor wire lined the top of the chain link fence that surrounded the parking lot. Security cameras covered every square inch of the campus. It was like working in Fort Knox.

In a mocking F.M. disc jockey voice he said out loud as if he had his own radio show, he recited one of his companies' radio commercials,

"Midland Bank. No fees! No hassles! No Problem!"
Fuck Midland. They should rewrite it to say,
"Mildand Bank. No pay! No Benefits! No life!"

Since leaving his apartment complex a thick fog had shrouded the valley leaving a quarter mile of visibility. Traffic was not too bad and he was making all the lights. It looked like he would make it to work with a minute or two to spare.

The closer he got to work the thicker the fog became. Visibility was down to less than a tenth of a mile. It was like driving into a cloud bank as he turned his car onto Midland Bank Way. His office building was eerily cloaked in fog making it invisible from the parking lot.

As he pulled up to the black steel electronic gate protecting the entrance to the parking lot to his building he grabbed his security badge. Jeremy opened his window, reached out and swiped his badge over an electronic sensor at the top of a black post next to his car. The eight-foot high black steel gate with black iron bars began to creek and buzz as it slowly began to rise off the ground. It was like a massive black railroad gate minus the red flashing lights and railroad crossing signs.

After it opened and locked in a vertical position, Jeremy drove slowly through the gate and into the parking lot. His favorite parking spot underneath a majestic oak tree was open. He parked, opened the car door, got out, closed the door and stood silently beside his car looking back at his office building.

Jeremy shivered and goose bumps ran up and down his arms as he watched the fog roll across the office complex campus grounds. The fog seemed to be a life form of its own. Floating just above the lawn like a ghost. One moment billowing like white smoke the next, dissipating, allowing him to see the entry way.

A deep feeling of dread sat in the pit of his stomach as he began to walk towards the door to his building. As the fog engulfed him he thought to himself,

"Oh, my God. This is like in the movie, The Exorcist, when the priest arrives in a taxi outside the little girl's house."

With or without the fog, every morning was like this for Jeremy. The feeling of dread and the deep despair and hopelessness tormented his every step as he walked toward his building

Some days he wanted to turn and run back to his car and never come back but he had debt. He had child support to pay. He had rent. He had to eat.

He swiped his security badge over the sensor located on the door frame to the entrance of the building. The door buzzed and he pulled the door open and walked into the lobby and towards the guard station twenty feet from the entry way.

The guard was a fifty-year old African American male name Brandon, who Jeremy thought looked like the actor Morgan Freeman. He stood six feet tall and weighed around 160 pounds. The hint of grey in his Black curly hair gave him an air of sophistication. His face looked like the surface of the moon as it was filled with deep pock marks and freckles. He wore a light blue button-down long-sleeved dress shirt that was two sizes too big. His black dress pants and belt, spit shined dress shoes were immaculate.

Brandon had worked security for fifteen years. He was a very quiet man and rarely spoke to anyone except when it came time for Jeremy to badge into the office. Brandon would almost immediately start to laugh.

Jeremy grabbed his security badge with his right hand and unsnapped it from his waist band and raised it up out in front of him so Brandon could see his picture and start to laugh but Brandon was preoccupied texting someone on his cell phone and only offered a brief glance at his badge. Jeremy quipped,

"Hey Brandon! What gives? You're not going to mock my picture today?"

"Sorry Jeremy. That fog is doing me in today. My baby's mama got into a really bad accident on the way to work. Human Resources said I could go and see her in the hospital but our fabulous CEO, Mr. Reed, told them that I can't leave to go see her in the hospital because she's not direct family. I swear to God that man is a living, breathing, drooling asshole."

"Damn! I am sorry to hear that. It's thick as pea soup out there. Is she ok?"

"Not sure. Her left leg is broken and she's got a sore neck. The paramedics took her to the E.R. She's been texting me from there. Some asshole slammed into her from behind. It's killing me knowing she's in pain and I can't be with her. Mr. Reed could have found someone else to cover for me."

"I hear you. He's a complete dick. They won't let us off the phones even to take a crap. One of the girls on my team, Janet, she got fired for missing her shift when she went to her father-in-law's funeral. The company didn't consider him immediate family either."

"It's tough here."

"Hope your wife is ok. I've got to get to my desk or the axe is going to fall for me too."

"Take care."

Jeremy turned to his right and walked thirty feet to the entrance of a long dimly lit hallway. The hallway was 150 feet long and lined with unlit, unoccupied small 10 foot by 10-foot conference rooms. Each conference room was filled with empty desks, chairs, filing cabinets and cubical walls stacked on top of one another. Remnants of former employee's desks had been shoved into these rooms after the companies last restructuring.

220 employees were laid off at the end of the previous quarter and their desks were shoved into the conference room when Midland Bank sublet the space that they use to occupy to another company.

The nauseating green glow of fluorescent lights radiated from the call center at the end of the hall. As Jeremy walked in the darkened hallway towards the light he felt as if a demonic green vortex was sucking him into an abyss. It was like one of those television shows where a person describes their near-death experience and going towards the light after some horrific car accident. In their stories the light these people described always represented heaven. It was warm, peaceful and welcoming. But the light that he walked towards seemed to pulsate like a cauldron of green swamp gas. He was walking into a mental and emotional torture chamber.

As he came closer to the entry to the call center the sound he heard made him break into a cold sweat. He could hear the distant muffled yet discernable voices of the call center employees answering their phones. Elaina's high pitched, almost falsetto voice, always stood out above the din of voices. Every time she answered the phone her tone went up at the end of the sentence.

"Thank you for calling Midland BANK. My Name is Ee-l-A ina…How can I make your day a happier one?"
It was pure torture to sit anywhere near her and listen to her talk on the phones.

Thirty feet before the entrance to the call center and to Jeremy's left was the men's restroom. To his right was a small break room with two small chintzy microwave ovens sitting on a narrow countertop next to a Bunn Low Automatic Coffee Brewer. Two traditional white kitchen refrigerators stood next to the counter. In the corner was a round counter top table with two red plastic chairs.

He was fortunate enough to have 10 minutes before he had to log into his phones and start taking calls so, he walked into the kitchen to grab a cup of coffee. He grabbed a Styrofoam cup from the stack of cup on the kitchen counter and then picked up the glass coffee pot. As he started to pour the coffee he noticed that nothing was coming out. Someone had left the coffee pot on the over the weekend and the coffee had burned into a charred solid mass stuck to the bottom of the pot.

In frustration he said to himself,

"Stupid fuckers left the pot on all weekend. Well, I still have time to take a dump."

Jeremy did an about face and walked out of the kitchen, across the hall an into the men's room. As he swung the door open he was immediately hit in the face with the stench of stale urine and the acrid smell of urinal blocks deodorizers.

Covering his nose, he stepped into the restroom and turned towards the urinals and saw a sticky yellow film covering the tile floor beneath both. Paper towels and toilet paper from the overflowing trash can were strewn about the floor. With his mouth and nose still covered with one hand he exclaimed,

"God damn cleaning people didn't come in over the weekend. What the fuck? Can't anyone do their jobs anymore?"

He reached for the handle to the door of the handicapped bathroom stall and pulled but the door was locked. He then heard snoring coming from the other

24

side of the door. One of his co-workers had decided to take a nap in the can. He swung open the door to the adjacent stall and began to step inside and but he was stopped in his tracks when he saw that the toilet seat was smeared with excrement.

He pounded on the wall to the handicapped stall and screamed,

"Wake up you-stupid fuck. I've got to take a shit!"

Without waiting for a response from the squatter, he walked to the door of the men's room, flung open the door and quickly walked out to go to his desk so he could log into the phones and start taking calls.

5 the call center

The corporate call center.

Considered by most who have labored in one to be a modern day sweat shop.
A dark and foreboding world permeated by the overwhelming stench of dread,
despair and hopelessness. These modern-day work camps are large windowless
cinderblock fortresses containing thousands of three foot by four-foot cubicles
where tormented, underpaid and overworked employees are tethered to their
work stations by the thin wire of their Plantronics headset. Hour after hour they
toil taking calls from desperate, enraged customers who circle their prey.
Modern day customers are kindred to a school of frenzied sharks desperately
probing the waters for the faintest scent of blood. Once any weakness is
discovered in the customer service representative they pounce and go in for the
kill demanding reparations for perceived wrongs done to them by the evil
corporation that they have agreed to do business with.

The air thick with the musty smell of body odor masked by the bittersweet smell
of cheap cologne makes it difficult to breath. Buzzing fluorescent lights
anchored above in the water stained drop ceiling tiles cast an eerie green glow
making the employees skin appear to be in various states of decomposition.

Boiling hot in the summer, freezing cold in the winter the climate is more than
most can take. Flu and upper respiratory infections spread like wildfire among
the staff causing many to miss up to a week of work at a time.

The Stress and tension to perform and meet the daily performance metrics
weighs heavy on the hearts and minds of every employee. Employees collapse
on regular basis after they reach their breaking point. The local paramedics can
be seen on a regularly wheeling their gurney complete with oxygen tanks and
cardio paddles into the building and onto the call center floor to save another
victim from life on the phones.

Midland Bank's call center is no different. Stretching out as far as the eye can see is an ocean of tiny cubicles. One quarter of the desks are filled with tormented souls taking calls. The other three quarters of the cubicles had been empty for several months. After Midland merged with a smaller competitor each desk was hastily abandoned during the layoff of several hundred employees.

The remaining cubicles are occupied by pale skinned zombies who once resembled men and women. The dark circles beneath their sunken eyes inflicted upon them from staring into the blue glow of computer screens for eight to ten hours a day. For ten-dollars an hour they sit tethered to their desks and are not permitted to move from their seat without permission. They are not permitted to speak to their co-workers.

After leaving the men's room Jeremy waded through row after row of cubicles until he arrives at his desk, cubicle number 44. Grey four-foot-high tweed fabric walls surround three sides of his desk. The fourth side opens into a narrow four-foot wide aisle. Jeremy has just enough room to roll back his chair without running into his co-worker seated directly behind him.

Many of his co-workers have decorated their cubicle walls with family photos, keep sakes, posters and trinkets. Most decorate to give them a sense of escape from this dull and drab corporate dungeon. One gentleman covered every square inch of his walls with prints of paintings by Rembrandt, van Gogh. Aside from a printout of telephone extensions pinned to his wall, Jeremy's walls were blank.

Each business quarter the company hires thirty new employees to man the phones. After a brief two-week training class where each recruit must learn the entire portfolio of thirty banking products and all 15 computer systems they are thrown onto the phones to take calls with little or no supervision. After two weeks of taking calls ten to fifteen of the new employees will no longer be with the company. The pressures of the job as well as the strict phone metrics and attendance policy will force employees to either resign or get fired. Many employees are never seen or heard from again after leaving for the day at the end of the previous day's shift. No, they aren't kidnapped or murdered, they simply refuse to come back to work the following day without a letter of resignation.

Chicken wire and sheet of plastic sags from the ceiling above Jeremy's desk to secure sagging ceiling tiles. It was put in place to protect him from falling debris. One night in Augusts a torrential downpour brought three inches of rain in one hour. The call center roof could not handle the large amount of water causing roof and drop ceiling above Jeremy's desk to give way sending a cascade of rainwater onto his desk. This destroyed his and several other employees' cubicles and computers. It was now November and maintenance had yet to fix the roof or the ceiling tiles. Jeremy always thought it was amusing that this was the only way he could get management to approve his supervisors requisition for his once archaic computer and monitor.

After sitting down at his desk, he closed his eyes and took ten deep soothing breaths to embrace his one last vestige of peace and quiet. In his mind, he pictured himself sitting beside his mother on a blanket beneath a large willow tree along the shores of Big Creek Lake. Big Creek was in a local metro park. It was place of sanctuary for he and his mother during her final days of a long battle with lung cancer. It was there that his mother would reflect upon her life. She talked of her hopes, her regrets and of her fear of dying. It was under the willow tree that she apologized for not giving him a better life. Today Jeremy's thoughts took him to of one of the last days he spent with his mother at their favorite spot. It was a beautiful and sunny Saturday afternoon. She was very weak and her breathing had become labored. She wheezed as she struggled to speak while disclosing to him what a beautiful-young man she thought he had turned out to be. Desperate to make up for the previous 26 years of pain and poverty he had endured with her she clutched his arms and looked deep into his eyes will telling him that she loved him more than anything in the world and wouldn't have traded him for anything.

It had been 20 years since she had passed but often reflected on this one moment with his mother to bring him peace. This one moment warmly stands out because she was not one to apologize or to show affection. Throughout his entire childhood, he had been told he would never amount to much but in her final days she began to reflect on her own life and how she had let herself and he son down.

The beautiful and serene visit with his mother was shattered by a single computerized tone filling the earpiece of his headset. Crashing back to reality his heart began to pound in his chest as recited his corporate introduction:

"Thank you for calling Midland Bank. My Name is Jeremy…How can I make your day a happier one?"

"What is your name, Jerry?"

"No sir. It's Jeremy. May I have your full name and account number please?"

"Whatever. My account number is 040711876."

"Thank you, sir. Unfortunately, that's your routing number. Can I have your full name and account number please?"

"Jerry. Listen. You want to make my day a happier one? I want these fucking fees waived and I want them waived now!"

"Sir. I am more than happy to help you with your account. How about your social security number? If you give me that I can look up your account information."

"My social security number. I ain't given that to you. I want your supervisor?"

"Sir, I am more than happy to help you with your account but I have no way to look at your fees unless I am able to pull up your account information and identify you."

"Yes. Are you stupid or something? Get me your god damn supervisor!"

"Yes, sir. May I tell her what it's regarding?"

"Ain't you listening fuck-tard. I am calling about the fees on my account."

"Sir. I'd be happy to get my supervisor for you but she will need your account number as well. May I have your name and account number please?"

"Jerry, I don't want to speak to you. Get me your supervisor now or is that too complex for you to understand?"

"It will be just moment. Please hold while I get her on the line."

"Hold? You people always want to put me on hold. Ok. But don't make me wait too long or I'll take my concerns to your CEO! Do you hear me son?"

Jeremy did not respond to the customer belittling him. He simply pressed the hold button on his telephone base station, took off his head set and pulled out his iPhone leaned back in his chair and started playing his favorite video game, Zombie Quest II. After a minute or two he stood up and look across the room to see if his supervisor, Christine, was at her desk. As usual, she was not there. On the other side of the wall was his buddy Drake. Jeremy stood up and leaned over the cubicle wall and said,

"Hey Drake. Are you on a call?"

Drake, immersed in a video game on his iPhone, responded in a dazed a faraway voice,

"No, Dude. I have this dick on hold. What's up?"

"It's supervisor time. Can you take a call? Christine's not at her desk."

Drake put down his phone and said,

"Hold on. Let me get rid of this guy and I'll take the call."

Drake took his customer off hold and said,

"Sorry for the wait sir. It will only be another moment."

He then disconnected the call and said to Jeremy,

"Transfer him on over."

Jeremy put his head set back on cleared his throat, pressed brought the customer back on line and said,

"Thank you so much for holding. I am going to transfer you to Drake. He's my supervisor and he'll be glad to take care of you today.

After Jeremy transferred the call he heard Drake answer his phone,

"This is Drake. I am a supervisor with Midland Bank. How may I help you today sir?"

"Well, Mr. Drake. I have fees on my account that I want waived and your stubborn ass customer service rep Jeremy didn't want to waive them for me."

"Oh, I am sorry to hear you have concerns about your account may I have your account number please?"

"God damn. I don't have my account number son. Can't you identify me some other way. How about my address or my date of birth?"

"Now sir. I understand your frustration but the only way I can pull up your account is with your account number or your social security number. May I have either one of them."

"You're giving me the same bullshit that Jerry was giving me. I'll give you my name, how about that?"

"Ok. Sir, what's your first and last name?"

The customer cleared his throat and replied,

"Bradley Foremen."

"Thank you, Mr. Foremen. What's your address?"

"It's 1684 Girdled Street. Ashlon, Ohio. 44067."

"Thank you, sir. I see your account here I will just need to identify you on the account. Please provide me with your password."

"Drake. Listen to me son. I don't remember my God Damn password. Can't you identify me in some other way?

Drake leaned forward with his elbows on his desk as he responded,

"Sir. I appreciate your concern. However, without your password I will have to direct you to your local branch. Make sure you take your driver's license with you. Any one of our tellers will be able to help you out with your account. Is there anything else I can help you with?"

"How about you suck my dick Drake?"

"Sir, unfortunately, I don't swing that way. I am afraid I am going to have tell you to go fuck yourself and disconnect our call."

"Why you som-bitch..."

Drake hit the release button on his base station and hung up on Mr. Foreman. He put his phone in "not ready" so he wouldn't receive any calls, stood up and leaned over his cubical wall and said to Jeremy,

"He's gone. Dude couldn't verify his password so I sent him to the branch. God damn. What a dick that guy was. Told me to suck his dick so, I told him to go fuck himself."

"Thanks Drake. I appreciate it. God damn these customers are complete ass hats."

Midland Bank, located in Akron, Ohio, had been in business for over 150 years. It serviced consumer accounts in Ohio, West Virginia, Pennsylvania and Kentucky. Some of their dedicated customer base had been banking with them for over 50 years. Even though the bank had a stronghold in the area as a trustworthy and competent financial institution they were a bit thrifty when it came to upgrading their computers and network to something even close to resembling the 21st century.

Jeremy had two systems. One was Outlook for sending and receiving email. The other was an ancient mainframe DOS based system. To pull up a customer's account he had to put a variety of codes into the entry field. DDA, F1, enter customers account number, then PPL then hit enter just to pull up the customers basic account information. He found it maddening but he loved this call center because they were so technologically backwards that they had no way to record the conversations that he was having with each customer and they had no way to record the screen shots of what he was looking at while on the phone with his customers. So, unless a supervisor was close by no one would know when he put on his "supervisor hat". There was virtually no way to grade him on his calls.

He and Drake went on what was considered an unauthorized break buy logging out of their phones. They walked to the breakroom located on the other side of the call center. It was a leisurely five-minute walk that gave them time to talk. The breakroom was cramped windowless room with a sink, two tables, two industrial sized refrigerators, a vending machine for snacks and another for soda. The room was so small that most people didn't spend much time in there. It was better than sitting and taking calls.

Drake was a 26-year-old musician and an ominous figure. He stood six-foot four inches tall with purple spiked hair and weighed 250 pounds. His arms were veiled in tattoos of skulls with blood dripping from the eye sockets. They sat down at a table in the corner of the room.

"Thanks for helping me with that call. I don't know about these customers. I am not sure I can take working here much longer."

Without looking up from his iPhone Drake replied,

"Same shit different day. I feel for you. These customers are driving me crazy too."

"What's up with these morons? They are calling us, their bank, and they won't give us their account number or social. They are clueless. We can see all that information when we pull up their account. It's not like we are going to steal their identities."

"I know. Most of them don't even have any money in their accounts and I bet that their credit is so bad that if either of us stole their identity we could do anything with it."

As Drake swiped at his phones screen a few times he said,

"Wouldn't it be great to just show up at one of their houses and kick their asses?"

"Trust me, it has crossed my mind more than once. How's your job at McDonalds going?"

"Dude it sucks. I am telling you, working both jobs is killing me but once I got Victoria pregnant I had to take this job to have benefits. I am determined to provide for my girl and my son."

"You know it's a boy?"

"Yeah. Victoria and I went in to her doctor on my day off and they did an ultrasound and it's a boy."

"Congrats! Really. That's some good news."

"I guess. Having two jobs is killing me. I can't even imagine what it's going to be like having a kid on top of everything else."

"You can do it. How about posting out for a new position here that pays more money so you can quit the job a McDonalds?"

"I wish. My numbers here aren't good enough. They won't let me post out until I meet all the minimum requirements. I get close to making them and Christine always seems to get me for some small infraction like returning late from one of my breaks. It's sucks."

"That's the way it works in every call center I have ever worked in. They trap you in the same position by nit picking at everything you do on the phones so you never get the scores you need to post out of your current position."

"It really sucks. Dude, this isn't your usual time for break, is it?"

"No. I just went into not ready to get away from the phones for a few minutes."

"You really crack me always working the system."

"If I don't I'll go crazy. Two 15-minute breaks and a half hour lunch isn't enough time off the phones. So, I give myself extra breaks. Christine talks to me about hit but she has never written me up."

"I would give myself additional break but I am afraid of losing this job with a kid on the way."

"Trust me. They won't fire you. They need bodies on the phones to handle the massive call volume. As long as you don't do it all the time you'll be fine."

"Hey! I love that new Little Black Book app you're selling on iTunes? I bought and downloaded it a few weeks ago. It's really cool how it's hidden from the main screen until you enter a separate password. It's even cooler that the addresses inside are encrypted until you enter an additional password. I feel like James Bond when I am using it. "

"Thanks for the support. How did you know about it? How did you know I created it?"

"One day I went to your desk to ask you a question about an account. I was standing behind you looking over your shoulder and I saw you tinkering with it while you were on the phone with a customer. That night I went home and looked up the developer on Google."

"But it's under my business name, Skating Bear Studios. How did you know I owned that business?"

"My old man was a detective for 35 years with the Akron P.D. So, snooping is in my DNA. I did some research on United States Patent and Trademark Office and there before my eyes was the name, Jeremy Grant of Akron, Ohio."

"I have it for sale on Amazon, iTunes and Google Play. What platform did you buy it from?"

"Google play. How's it going? How many have you sold?"

"Enough to generate the equivalent of a part-time job. I am not going to get rich but it pays for what this job doesn't."

"Why did you create it? Who are your clients?"

"I designed it for people in relationships whose hearts have wandered. They are cheating on their significant other and want to keep prying eyes out of their business, especially divorce attorneys. The app is designed to be fail safe. Once the user logs out of the app it becomes invisible. It fades from the screen of the phone. Only the user knows where it's stored and how to access it. If anyone who doesn't have the passcode tries to gain access three times in a row the app implodes. It self-destructs and disappears from the phone and all its contents are permanently deleted. Not even the sharpest FBI forensic data recovery experts can recover the data that was contained in it.

"It's really cool how the app is invisible until you touch the section of the screen where it is located and then it slowly reappears."

"I am glad you like it. I really appreciate your support. So, are you stalking me or just a nosey detective's son?

"No need to worry. I was just snooping around."

Well, I am going to get back on the phones."

"Hey! Before you go, there's this customer by the name of Mr. Rodansky that keeps calling in. He can't answer any of the security questions on his account so we haven't been able to answer the questions he has on his account. He keeps hanging up and calling back in thinking the next customer's service representative is going to help him. He gets angrier and angrier with each call. Just watch out for him."

Ok. See you in a few. Take care."

6 the little black book

Thank you for calling Midland Bank. My Name is Jeremy. How can I make your day a happier one?"

The customer on the other end of the line coughed and cleared his throat but did not respond."

Jeremy repeated his greeting,

"Thank you for calling Midland Bank. My Name is Jeremy…How can I make your day a happier one?"

At the end of the line Jeremy could hear a man peeing into a toilet. The toilet flushed and then there was silence.

Jeremy asked,

"Is anyone on the line?"

The man on the other end of the line cleared his throat and in a deep monotone voice he said,

"It's not cool to be made to wait is it Jeremy?"

"Sir?"

"Do you have any idea how long I was on hold before you answered the line? Do you?!"

"No sir. I apologize. I am happy to help you. May I have your name and account number please."

Jeremy heard the crackling sound of burning tobacco as the customer taking a deep drag off a cigarette. He exhaled the smoke as he spoke,

"My account number is 34768912. My name is Rodansky. Jako Rodansky."

"Thank you, Mr. Rodansky. I have your account pulled up. For security purposes may I have your password?"

"Oh, god damn it! I don't remember that. Can't you ask me something else."

"Unfortunately, Mr. Rodansky, you called in a while ago and asked not to give anyone access to your account unless they gave us your password."

"Can you give me a hint"

"Unfortunately, I am unable to provide a hint. I am going to have to refer you to your local branch if you don't know your password."

Mr. Rodansky's voice became strained as he replied,

"Jeremy, listen to me. I am not going to my local branch. You're going to give me some information on my account so I don't have to do that. Do you understand me?"

"Mr. Rodansky, I truly understand your frustration but without your password we are not permitted to give anyone access to your account. If you have access to a computer and the internet you can get information on your account there."

Mr. Rodansky remained silent for a few moments before he replied.

"Jeremy, I don't have internet access and I don't have a computer. If I have to go to the branch to get basic information on my account it's not going to be good."

"Sir, what do you mean it's not going to be good?"

"Well, I was on hold for almost an hour, I finally get through and get to speak to you only to have you tell me you won't give me access to my own account. Do you have any idea how far away the nearest branch is Jeremy? It's a 45-minute drive and my mother is dying of cancer and I've got to go see her in the hospital. If you make my life any more complicated than it already is I am not going to the branch but I am coming down to your call center. I know where you're located on Midland Bank Way."

"Mr. Rodansky, so, what are you saying?"

"Have you ever been in combat son?"

"Combat? Like, have I fought in Iraq?"

"You got it. Have you ever been in a combat situation?"

"Fortunately, no."

"Well you're about to find out what combat is like my friend."

Jeremy was seething on the inside but his mind became unexpectedly clear. He wasn't going to take it any more from this man or any other customer. A controlled rage bubbled from the bottom of his soul as he leaned forward with his elbows on the edge of his desk, closed his eyes and said in a calm, clear and stern voice,

"Mr. Rodansky, I'd be very careful making idol threats. You are aware that I have all your personal information sitting right in front of me on my computer screen, aren't you? I know where you live, how much money you have, your date of birth and your social security number.
I know where and when you shop, where you work and who your wife is. I even know that you frequent a gay dating website. I am sure your wife would love to know about that. Are you certain you have picked the right customer service representative to fuck with today?

There was no response from Mr. Rodansky only silence. After a moment, Jeremy heard a click and there was dial tone in his ear. He sat back and pulled out his iPhone and pulled up his app titled Little Black Book.

He clicked on it and it opened and asked for his password.

He entered his password and clicked on the K tab and clicked on the plus sign in the upper right-hand corner of the address book to enter a new contact. As he entered Mr. Rodansky's personal information he spoke out loud,

"Fucktard #32
Mr. Furcktard Rodansky. 10712 Alvion Rd. New Ryan, Ohio 44123.
Phone: 216-285-4341.
Email: brodansky@mymail.com
And let's see, for a note what can I put? That's it. He's a complete dickhead."

Jeremy saved Mr. Rodansky's information closed the Little Black Book application and opened Facebook. Clicking on the search field he entered, Jako Rodansky.

The first person who came up in the search results was an unshaven, chubby middle-aged man with tattoos of a bright green dragon on each arm, the head of each dragon was on the backside of each hand with yellow lizard like eyes with a diamond pupil looking up at the viewer. He had long greasy black hair and was wearing a black Harley Davidson T-Shirt. From, Cleveland, Ohio.

Jeremy said out loud,

"Bingo! There's the fat fuck. Let's see what kind of photo's, likes and friends he has."

Mr. Rodansky only had 30 friends. His profile contained only five pictures. One picture showed him on his Harley and another showed him at a bar with two friends. All three flipping the bird at the camera while their picture was taken.

"Classy bunch." Jeremy said to himself.

He put his phone into not ready, took off his headset got up from his desk. He wasn't sure who to discuss the conversation he had just had with his customer. First, he walked over to Christine's cubicle but she was not at her desk. So, he decided to talk to the Brandon the security guard about the conversation he just had with Mr. Rodansky.

As he approached Brandon he said,

"Hey there Brandon, I have another hot one for you."

Brandon rolled his eyes as he asked,
"Jeremy, not another customer threatening the blow up the call center?"

Jeremy chuckled as he responded,
"You betcha ya my friend. Every day is an adventure at Midland Bank."

Brandon brought up a 20 page excel spread sheet on his computer. The spreadsheet was titled:

POTENTIAL CORPORATE THREATS

It contained the names of hundreds of customers that Jeremy and other customers service representatives had brought to securities attention.

"Ok. Jeremy. What's his name, address and phone?"

"Mr. Furcktard Rodansky.
Sorry, that's Jako Rodansky

10712 Alvion Rd. New Ryan, Ohio 44123.
Phone? 216-285-4341.
Email? brodansky@mymail.com"

"Do you need anything else?"

"Nope. I've got Mr. Rodansky documented. We're all set. I'll call the police and give them a heads-up."

"Sure. Thanks."

Jeremy turned and deliberately walked slowly back to his desk to delay getting back onto the phones for another two or three minutes.
When he arrived at his desk there was a bright pink sticky note stuck to his computers screen.
Written on it was note from his supervisor Christine. It read.

"Jeremy, when your back to your desk please come see me."

As Jeremy sat down he said to himself,

"Oh God! What's this all about? She probably wants to go over my numbers."

Jeremy logged out of his phone and put it in Coaching. Coaching was a status for his phone when he wasn't taking calls and was in a formal meeting. As he spun around in his chair and started to get he was startled by Christine who was standing directly behind him.

Christine was rubenesque woman standing 5'11" and appeared physically a bit like the cartoon character Shrek in drag. Her greasy dishwater blond hair speckled with flecks of dandruff was always pulled back into a pony tail and secured by a black scrunchie. Every day she wore the same outfit: Faded and torn blue jeans, a black tank top with a pink cashmere sweater draped over her shoulders and light brown leather gladiator sandals with thin leather straps that tightly wound around and dug into her swollen ankles. The bitter musty smell of moth balls that radiated from her body made Jeremy gag He imagined that her stench she was from being held captive in a wooden storage container that had holes drilled in the top and sides to give her air to breathe. Maybe she was made to sleep on scraps of newspaper and fed pieces of carrots through a knot hole in the side of her cage and let out in the morning so she could go to work.

He looked up at her and said,

"Hey Christine. I just got back to my desk and saw your note. What's up?"

Christine nervously adjusted her sweater, crossed her arms across her chest and said,

"Jeremy, let's go into the Sunset meeting room. I need to go over a few things with you."

"Ok, Sure. There's nothing on the calendar for today is there?"

"No. I know. Something has come up and we need to talk."

Christine abruptly turned and began to walk to the back of the call center where there were four meeting rooms. Each had clever names such as The Sunrise, The Sunset, Moonrise and the Twilight meeting rooms. Supervisors and customer service representatives regularly met in these rooms for team meetings and to go over their call statistics.

Once they reached the doorway to the room Christine said,

"Go ahead inside and sit down."

Jeremy sat down at the table and asked,

"What's going on?"

As Christine sat down across the table from him Wanda the Human Resources representative appeared in the doorway. Wanda was a morbidly obese African American woman who was wider than she was tall. She had her left knee in a brace and it was propped up on a four-wheeled scooter that she pushed with a handle as she walked to support her massive frame.
Her lips were always painted bright red with lipstick. Much of it encrusted her upper teeth. She wore a gold betty page wig that appeared to small for her bulbous head. She wheezed as she rolled herself into the room and paused near the edge of the table.

Jeremy smirked as he welcomed her.

"Hi Wanda. What's going on?"

Wanda pushed her scooter to the other side of the table so she was next to Christine. The sound of her wheezing increased as she took a deep breath and began to speak,

"Jeremy, as you know, there have been some changes going on here at Midland. Due to the recent reorganization, there have been some budget changes put into place and unfortunately, for all of us, corporate has decided to close this call center down. Within the next 30 days all our positions will be eliminated, as many other positions, have been eliminated. All of our positions here in Akron are being outsourced to India."

Jeremy's jaw dropped open and he made a quiet choking sound. Then he said,

"No. No way!" They told us that wouldn't happen and our jobs were safe."

Wanda took a deep breath that made her massive chest heave as she replied,

"Jeremy, I am truly sorry. Unfortunately, that was not the case. We would like you to stay with us for the remaining thirty days to help complete the smooth transition to the new call center in India. After your final day, you will be given two-weeks' severance pay and of course you can apply for unemployment at the unemployment office. You will also get an email delivered to your personal email about getting health insurance through COBRA."

"You've got to be fucking kidding me Wanda. This can't happen right now. It just can't."

"Jeremy, I know this is tough but it's completely out of my hands. My job is going to be eliminated too. Are you willing to stay with us throughout the transition period?"

Jeremy felt numb. His thoughts began to race. He thought about how much he despised this job and had often prayed to get laid off or fired. But now that it was happening it didn't feel nearly as good as he thought it would. Sitting back in his chair he looked over Wanda's left shoulder and stared blankly out the window behind her and said,

"So, that's it. All this time with Midland and that's it. Two weeks' severance and a kick in the fucking ass and I am out of a job."

Wanda choked back tears as she said,

"Jeremy, I am truly sorry. Truly I am. I have three kids and am taking care of my mom. It's going to be rough for all of us. Please don't make this any harder that it has to be."

Jeremy's gaze didn't shift from the window as he replied,

"No, I won't make this difficult. Sure. I'll stay for the additional 30 days. I have to. I need the money."

"I know and we appreciate your support. You know you can count on me for a great reference in the future."

Christine stood up as Wanda pushed her scooter out of the meeting room door. Jeremy walked back to his desk and logged back onto the phones.

7 cracking up

"Thank you for calling Midland Bank. My name is Jeremy. How can I make your day a happier one?"

The male customer on the other end of the line cleared his throat and in a deep baritone voice said in a thick southern accent,

"Son, you can make my day a happier one if you can tell me why your God Damn bank has stuck me right in the ass with all-of-these God damn fees?"

Without hesitating Jeremy responded in warm friendly tone,

"I'd be happy to assist you with your concerns sir. May I have your account number so I can look at your account?"

"Jeremy, my account number is 23578693."

Jeremy entered the account number in to his system as he replied

"Thank you. May I have the name on the account?"

The customer hesitated, cleared his throat and said,

"It's Sally Jamerson."

"Thank you for that sir and what is your name?"

There was silence for a few seconds and Jeremy repeated his question,

"Sir? What is your name?"

"Jeremy, my name is Robert Randolph. I am Mrs. Jamerson's son."

"Thank you, Mr. Randolph. Unfortunately, I don't show you listed on this account as a signer. Is Mrs. Jamerson available. I can get her identified and then if she gives me permission to speak to you on her account I'd be happy to help you."

Agitated Mr. Randolph responded,

"Listen Jeremy. My mother is in a coma at The Cleveland Clinic and she is unable to come to phone. I just need you to tell me why she is being charged all of these God damn fees. I know you don't know your ass from a hole in the ground but just tell me why there are all these fees on her account!"

As Jeremy surveyed Mrs. Jamerson's account he saw that she has $50,000 in her checking and over $200,000 in her savings as well has a several certificates of deposit totaling over $500,000.
The notes on her account that her son had called in several times attempting to gain access and Mrs. Jamerson does not want him to have access to her money.

"Mr. Randolph, I appreciate that. Unfortunately, since you are not a signer on the account I need to have you go to one of our local branches with your mother to have her add you to the account.
I apologize."

"Jeremy! You're not listening to me you shit for brains idiot. I just want to know why there are fees on her account. That's all. Why is that so hard for a retard like you to understand?!"

Jeremy's heart began to race and he closed his eyes. A furious rage started to build from deep within him. Rude and offensive customers were part of the job and he usually handled them with a professional demeanor. But over time the abuse had accumulated in his subconscious like a thick black tar. Today Mr. Randolph had pushed all the wrong buttons and he exploded with rage as he replied through clenched teeth,

"Mr. Randolph, you sound like an uneducated, whiskey swilling inbred hillbilly who's just trying to get into his mama's account so you can steal her money because you aren't capable of finding a job to support yourself. Did you drink yourself into poverty you fucking asshole?"

What Jeremy thought was static on the line was the sound of a loud twisted scream of rage coming from Mr. Randolph as he exclaimed,

"How fucking dare, you, you fucking punk. Get me your supervisor now. I'll make sure you lose your job for this. Do you hear me you fuck? Get me your super now!"

Sweat beads appeared on Jeremy's brow and he trembled as he replied,

"Beg me you redneck loser. Still sucking on mama's tittie aren't' you?"

Just as his words were coming out of his mouth the room began to spin and he was having trouble breathing. Jeremy ripped off his headset, stood up on his chair and screamed at the top of his lungs,

"Fuck this place. Fuck it. This place fucking sucks!"

His tirade was so loud that it echoed off the walls making every one of his co-workers spin around in their chairs to look at him in horror. The woman sitting next to him stood up, pulled off her headset and demanded,

"What's wrong with you!"

Jeremy jumped off his chair and ran down the aisle screaming,

"This place fucking sucks. I've got to get out of here. You've all got to get out of here before these customers kill you. Before they start showing up at your house and demand your soul from you while you sleep. Get out! Get out! Get out before it's too late! Don't let them swallow your soul."

He turned and ran down the hall and into the men's room and locked himself inside the handicapped stall. After Ripping off his clothes he sat naked, leaning forward with arms crossed on the toilette rocking back and forth repeating over and over,

"Get out! I've got to get out before it's too late. It's too late. It's too late."

After a few minutes the door to the men's room opened and Brandon the security guard came in.
He walked up to the door of the handicapped stall and quietly asked,

"Jeremy? Are you ok? People on the call center floor said you just flipped out and ran in here."

The only response he could hear through the walls of the stall was Jeremy stammering over and over,

"Get out! I've got to get out before it's too late. It's too late. It's too late."

Brandon replied,

"Hey Jeremy, I am not sure what you're talking about but the director of the call center is calling the cops. They are going to be hear any minute. Come on man. You don't want to let them take you like this."

Again, the only thing that Brandon could hear was Jeremy repeating over and over,

"Get out! I've got to get out before it's too late. It's too late. It's too late."

Brandon walked out of the restroom and was greeted by two uniformed police officers
standing outside in the hall.

Officers Eddy and Danforth had been called to this call center so many times that they were all on a first name basis with each other.

Officer Eddy said,

"Hey there Brandon. What's seems to be the issue today."

With a serious look of concern on this face. With his brow was furrowed he replied,

"Well, one of our employees, Jeremy Grant, he's locked himself in the handicapped stall in the men's room. Apparently, he flipped out and started screaming and yelling when he was on the phone in the call center. He ran in here and locked himself in the bathroom stall."

Officer Danforth responded,

"Sounds like he cracked up. We are going to need to call an ambulance to take him over to Heather Hill for evaluation.

Brandon looked at Officer Danforth and said,

"Heather Hill? That's the nut house over on the north side, isn't it?"

"Sure is. I'll call an ambulance if you guys want to try and get him out of the stall."

As officer Danforth turned to go back to the lobby, officer Eddy moved toward the bathroom door to go inside. Brandon stepped in front of him and said,

Hold on there, Eddy. Jeremy is a good guy. He's just a little stressed out. You're not really going to take him to the nut house?"

"Brandon, it sounds like he's having a break down. When the paramedics get here they'll check him out and probably take him to the E.R. first. The E.R. doctor will determine what happens to him after that."

"Ok, when we go inside just be nice to the guy."

"Ok, Brandon. We first have to see how to get him to open the bathroom stall door."

They both walked into the men's room and slowly moved towards the handicapped stall at the end of the room. They could both here Jeremy saying over and over,

"Get out! I've got to get out before it's too late. It's too late. It's too late."

Officer eddy walked up to the door of the stall and softly knocked on the door and said,

"Hey Jeremy? It's officer Eddy. What's going on? How are you doing?"

There was silence for a few moments and officer Eddy said,

"Jeremy? You not feeling so well? Open up the door so we can help you out. Everything's going to be ok."

There was a brief silence then Jeremy shouted,

"You're not taking me to jail. I haven't done anything wrong. You're not taking me to jail!"

Brandon responded,

"Hey Jeremy, it's me Brandon. They are not taking you to jail. They just want to make sure you're ok. We're going to have the paramedics take a look at you to make sure you're ok."

Jeremy began to cry as he said,

"Please! Please don't take me to jail. I don't want to go to jail. Just let me go back home."

Brandon replied,

"I promise you they are not going to take you to jail. Please open up the door so we can make sure you're ok. You've got to let me make fun of your security badge again. Come on bud."

They could hear Jeremy begin to move around. He began to sob as he opened the stall door. As it swung inward they could see him naked and wedged between the toilet and the wall of the bathroom. His cloths were draped over the toilet and on the floor. Officer Eddy said,

"Brandon, could you go outside and watch for the paramedics while I get Jeremy cleaned up?"

"Sure, Eddy."

As Brandon turned to leave there was a knock on the men's room door and a voice on the other side said,

"Paramedics. Is it ok to come in?"

Brandon on yelled,

"Yes. Please come in."

The door opened and in walked paramedics Stanley Lawrence and Jim Leeson.

Stanley said,

"What's the situation?"

Officer Eddy responded,

"We have an adult male by the name of Jeremy Grant Apparently, he's had some sort of breakdown or episode. He was locked in the stall back there but he just opened the door. He's taken off all of his clothes so we have to get him dressed."

Stanley asked,

"An episode?"

Officer Eddy replied,

"We think he's having a nervous breakdown of some sort. I guess he started yelling and ran in here and locked himself in the stall."

"Damn! We are called here at least once a month for stress related disorders. Is he violent? Has anyone checked him for weapons."

"He doesn't appear to be violent. No, I haven't even had a chance to talk with him yet. Let me chat with him and see how he's doing. I'll let you know if it's safe for you guys to take him out of here."

"Ok."

As officer Eddy cautiously walked towards the bathroom he called out to Jeremy,

"Hey Jeremy? It's officer Eddy. I just want to make sure you're ok so, I am going to come inside and talk to you ok?"

Jeremy was sobbing as he responded,

"Please don't arrest me. I don't want to go to jail."

Officer Eddy walked into the bathroom stall and touched Jeremy on the shoulder and said,

"Jeremy, looks like you're having a bad day. Don't worry, we're not going to take you to jail. I just want to make sure you're ok and that you don't have any weapons on you before the paramedics take a look at you. Ok?"

Jeremy sniffled and said,

"It's Ok. I don't have any weapons on me."

Officer Eddy slowly picked up the pants, shirt and underwear that were draped over the toilet and picked up his socks and shoes from the floor and asked,

"Do you have anything sharp that will poke me or anything illegal like drugs in your pockets?"

Jeremy quietly replied,

"No."

The only thing officer Eddy found was Jeremy's cloths, his wallet and security badge. He said to Jeremy who was naked and shivering on the bathroom floor,

"Jeremy, let me help you off the ground so the paramedics can take a look at you, ok?"

Jeremy's voice trembled as he replied,

"I guess so."

Jeremy pushed himself out from between the bathroom wall and the toilet as officer Eddy helped him to his feet. Jeremy wiped his mucous encrusted upper lip and chin with his right forearm as the two of them walked from the bathroom stall. They were greeted by paramedic Leeson who draped a white blanked over Jeremy's shoulders and said,

"You're really cold. Let's get you warmed up in the ambulance where we can check your vitals and get you to the hospital. Ok?"

"Ok. Just don't take me to jail."

"We're not. We're going to take you to Heather Hill Hospital. It's right down the road."

"Ok. You're a nice man. Thank you."

8 heather hill

Morning rays of sun light danced on the shear white curtain hanging over the solitary window on the south side of the Jeremy's hospital room as he started to wake up. Laying on his back, he strained to open his eyes. A mind shattering migraine made it feel as if his head had been split open with a hatchet.

Thinking he was at home and in his own bedroom he attempted to roll to his left to look at his alarm clock but he was unable to move. He attempted to reach up to rub his eyes but he could not move his arms.

His eye lids were as heavy as a boulder and it seemed impossible to keep them open. He attempted to swing his legs over the edge of the bed he but could not move them either. He could feel them but not move them. All he could do was lift his head from his pillow.

Jeremy's head throbbed as he struggled to raise it from the pillow. The room he was lying in slowly came into focus. He strained to view his surroundings through blurry eyes. As things gradually became clearer it was more than apparent that he was in a hospital bed. His hands and feet were tethered to their corresponding bed side rails with a thick white strap padded with fleece. Covering his body was a single white blanket. Hanging from the ceiling above the foot of his bed was a small flat screen television. Over his left shoulder and parallel to the bed was monitor sitting on top of a white medical hospital cart with all of his vital signs glowing like a Christmas tree in green, red and yellow.

To his left was a large plate glass window next to the open door to his room. Through the window, he could see a nurse sitting at the nurse's station. In a weak, raspy voice Jeremy called out to her,

"Hey! Nurse! Nurse! Where am I?"

Nurse Graves quickly got up and came into his room and walked to the side of his bed. As she studied his vitals on the monitor behind him she replied,

"Mr. Graves, you're at Heather Hill Hospital for observations. How are you feeling?"

Jeremy replied sarcastically,

"Is there an axe in my head?"

The nurse laughed,

"No. No axes. We had to sedate you last night. You were in pretty bad shape when they brought you in. The sedative we gave you is known to give patients a pretty bad hang over."

"Bad shape? What happened?"

"Let me have Dr. Gupta go over that with you. He's making his rounds now and should be in any minute."

"Can you untie me? I've really got to go to the bathroom."

"You're fine for now. We inserted a catheter in your urinary tract. So, if you have to urinate it's going into a bottle on the side of your bed. As far as a bowel movement that's why we have bed pans. Do you need the bed pan?"

"No. It just feels like I have to take a leak really bad."

"Let's wait for Dr. Gupta and see what he has to say."

"Am I in the emergency room?"

Nurse Graves pause and then replied,

"No. Actually you're in the psychiatric ward at Heather Hill."

"No fucking way! It looks like I went from one asylum to another."

"Were you a patient at another psychiatric ward before being admitted to Heather Hill?"

"You might say that. I work in a call center in Midland Bank and it's the next best thing to a nut house."

Jeremy's voice began to trail as he closed his eyes. He quietly asked,

"Did I flip out at work?"

"Mr. Grant, that's what the report from the paramedics say. Let's wait until Dr. Gupta gets here to discuss the specifics. Why don't you get some more rest?"

"I think it's coming back to me. I was in the men's room at work and the next thing I know I am waking tied to the bed at Heather Hill."

Startling both Jeremy and the Nurse Graves in walked a small framed grey-haired man standing five feet tall, with thick framed glasses, wearing a white lab coat. He moved swiftly into the room and to the side of the bed. Speaking with an Indian accent he smiled and asked,

"Hello my friend. How are we feeling today?"

"Who the fuck-are you?"

He laughed as he replied,

"I am Dr. Ajeet Gupta and I am your admitting physician."

"Ajeet Gupta. What kind of name is that?"

Dr. Gupta threw his head back and laughed as he replied,

"Oh, my friend. I am from a far-away land called India. My name, Ajeet, is a Hindi name meaning, invincible but you may call me Bob. I am sure you have heard that more than once in your industry."

Jeremy didn't laugh but said,

"Oh, my God. I really am in the nut house."

"Well my friend, you were in serious shape last night. I wouldn't say you're in the "nut house. But you are in the psychiatric ward of Heather Hill Hospital. Nurse Graves, how is our friend doing this fine day?"

Nurse graves walked over to the monitoring equipment and looked at his vitals.

"Dr. Gupta, Mr. Grant's vitals are excellent. His blood pressure is one-twenty-five over ninety. His pulse is good as well. His blood work came back this morning and there were no intoxicating substances in his blood stream."

Dr. Gupta replied,

"Excellent. Mr. Jeremy, your vitals are back to normal. Nurse. Graves please excuse Mr. Jeremy and I while we have a chat. Ok?"

"Yes, Dr. Gupta."

Nurse Graves left the room and returned to her station. Dr. Gupta pulled up the chair sitting against the wall next to his bed and sat down. He smiled as he asked,

"Mr. Jeremy, what do you remember from yesterday?"

"All I remember was talking to a paramedic in the men's room at work. I thought he was going to take me to jail for some reason."

"My friend, from what the report says and how you were acting when they brought you into the emergency room, we believe you had what we call a psychotic episode also known as a nervous breakdown. Have you been under a lot of stress?"

"I work in a call center. There's almost always insurmountable amounts of stress. I have devoted myself to that place and yesterday I found out that they will be eliminating my position. What am I going to do?"

"From what the report said you started screaming, ran into the men's room and barricaded yourself in one of the stalls. You begged the paramedics not to take you to jail. Do you have any idea why you think they would take you to jail?"

"None whatsoever. Maybe I thought I had broken some sort of law."

"Well, none that I am aware of. Maybe disturbing the peace or disorderly conduct but there are no laws against having a psychotic episode. More often than not these types of episodes are triggered by extreme mental pressures, fatigue or bouts with guilt. Often times the guilt is fueled by feelings of remorse, regret and extreme life circumstances or changes such as loss of a job. But loss of a job by itself doesn't usually trigger such extreme reactions. It's usually a combination of extreme circumstances."

Jeremy stared blankly at the rays of sunlight dancing across the curtains covering his window and said,

"Doc. Could you please untie me from the bed?"

Dr. Gupta smiled as he replied,

"You don't remember last night in the emergency room. Do you?"

"Like I told you, the last thing I remember is talking to a paramedic in the men's room. Next thing I know I am waking up here, tied to the bed."

"Mr. Jeremy, I will have nurse Graves release you from your restraints but you have to promise not to threaten that you are going to gouge out my eyes and shit in their empty sockets. We had to have several staff member restrain you and give you very strong sedative,"

"Forgive me. If I said something like that I was out of my mind. Please let untie me."

"Let's get nurse Graves in here so she can get you up and moving again. If you get out of line at all I am going to recommend that we have you sent to Sheppard Health Services for further evaluation."

"Doc, that's the nut house up on the hill. I have heard horror stories about that place."

"Well, let's hope we don't have to go to those extremes for your psychological assessment."

Dr. Gupta stood up, patted Jeremy on the shoulder and returned the chair he had been sitting in, to its original resting place against the wall and walked out of the room to the nurse's station.

Jeremy watched the doctor and nurse Graves have a short but serious discussion. Dr. Gupta walked away. After a few minutes three large muscular male orderlies appeared at the nurse's station. Nurse Graves and the three orderlies entered the room. She stood in the corner of the room, crossed her arms over her chest and said in a strict authoritarian tone,

"Mr. Grant, my staff is going to release you from your restraints. If you show any signs of aggressive behavior towards myself or any of these men we will have no choice but to sedate you and restrain you to the bed again. As doctor Gupta stated, we will also look at having you admitted to Sheppard Health Services for further evaluation. Do I make myself perfectly clear?"

"It doesn't get much clearer. I see you brought the big guns just in case I get out of line."

"Mr. Grant, I am more than happy to show you the security video of your interactions with our staff yesterday evening."

"No need for that but did anyone ever tell you your beautiful when you're being strict?"

"Let's see what you say when I remove your catheter."

Nurse Graves reached into the pocket of her lab coat and removed two rubber surgical gloves. After pulling a glove onto each hand she stepped to the right side of Jeremy's bed and pulled back the white blanket covering his body. She then pulled up his linen hospital gown exposing his lower abdomen and genitalia.

Protruding from the mouth of his penis was a four-foot-long quarter inch thick transparent plastic tube. It stretched to his right and emptied into a plastic receptacle bag hanging on the lower frame of his bed. The hose was partially filled with fresh streams of urine which had dripped from Jeremy's bladder overnight.

Jeremy pulled against his arm restraints as nurse Graves firmly grabbed his semi flaccid penis with her left forefinger and thumb. He quipped sarcastically,

"God damn! You're not going to give me a hand job right in front of these gentlemen, are you?"

She did not respond. She moved her right hand down the mouth of his penis and placed her thumb and for finger on the plastic tube stemming from urethra and said,

"This is going to pinch a bit."

As she slowly started to pull on the tube to remove it from his urinary tract Jeremy flinched severely and pulled at his arm and leg restraints as he yelped in pain,

"Oh, my fucking God. What did you just do to me?"

With a wicked grin on her face she said,
"I removed your catheter. I told you it was going to pinch. If we were alone I would have given you a hand job but without a happy ending. Untie him from the bed and get me a wheel chair so I can take him to the atrium for some fresh air."

The three men released Jeremy's hands and legs from their bonds. One of the men left the room and returned with a wheel chair. He rolled it to the left side of Jeremy's bed and said,

"Is there anything else we can assist you with today Nurse Graves?"

"No. That's all. You've been a big help. Please stay near by just in case he gets out of hand again."

The orderlies left the room.

Nurse Graves pulled his hospital down and help him sit up on the side of his bed.

"How are you feeling Mr. Grant?"

As Jeremy slowly reached up with both hands and rand his fingers through his hair he said,

"I don't know. I don't know what hurts worse, my head or my penis."

"Sorry about that. There's no easy way to remove a catheter. Thank God you were out of it when we put it in you. Let's get you into the wheel chair and to the atrium where we can get you some fresh air."

She stepped in front of Jeremy, locked the breaks on the wheel chair and helped him slowly slide off the edge of the bed to a standing position. Draped over her arm was a white linen bath robe.

"Here. Put on this robe. The Atrium is a little drafty and this will keep you warm."

Jeremy slowly slid his arms into the robe and ted the belt around his waist. Nurse Graves helped him into the wheel chair.

"How are you feeling?"

"My head is pounding and I feel dizzy but I think I am ok."

"Ok. Let's go for a ride. I think you need to meet some of your hospital mates."

Nurse Graves steered the wheel chair through the door and past the nurse's station.

Jeremy asked,

"Did you say you were taking me to the atrium? What is the atrium."

It's a room located on the top floor of the hospital where many of our patients go to reflect, relax and recover. It's a very quiet and very peaceful setting that I believe will do someone like yourself a lot of good.

Peter Tompkins

9 the shooting range

Drake pulled into the parking lot and parked his navy blue 1989 Buick Lesabre Custom four door sedan in the spot next to the handicapped spot near the front entrance of the range. He grabbed his desert camouflaged back pack containing his Glock 17, several boxes of ammo and a few custom targets he had designed at home on his computer and got out of his car. After slinging the back pack over his left shoulder, he opened the door to the range and walked in.

After approaching the counter to pay for his time Jeffery, of the clerks called out,

"Hey there Drake. Going to do some shooting today?"

"You bet Jeffery. Set me up for an hour. I've got a lot to shoot about."

"I hear ya. That'll be $30.00."

"No problem. As he paid he asked,

"Is my favorite station open tonight? Number 9?"

"Yes sir. It's been waiting for you all night. Here's your earmuff's and eye protection. Do you need any targets?"

"Nope. I brought my own this time. Something I came up with on the computer at home."

Jeffery laughed as he said,

"Sounds Good. Have a good shoot."

Drake stepped to his left and approached a large, windowless steel door. On the other side of the door was an indoor shooting range with ten shooting booths. It was a large room fifty yards long and forty yards wide with white walls and grey floors. At the far end of the firing lanes the floor was the bullet trap where the floor was angled up towards the ceiling. Each stall was painted gun metal grey and had a small tray suspended above the floor. This was where shooters placed their ammunition and firearms.

After opening the door, Drake walked to the second to last station to his right and placed his backpack on the floor and pulled his Glock 17, a box of ammo and his target. After putting on his earmuffs and eye protection he placed two loaded magazines on the tray. Raising the home-made target above his head he clipped it to the guiding wire hanging from the ceiling above and said out loud,

"Mr. Rodansky, this bullet's for you."

The target was twenty-three inches wide and thirty-five inches long. Printed in the center was a black and white picture of one of his customers. Them was a heavy-set white, unshaven middle-aged man with greasy black hair. Drake had downloaded the picture the gentleman's Facebook page. He sent the target twenty-yards down range on the wire.

Pulling back on the slide he chambered his first round, took aim and slowly squeezed the trigger. The boom from the gun echoed off of the walls. As the bullet struck, the target bend inward and swayed in the air for a moment and then became still. Drake lowered his weapon to admire his marksmanship.

"Bullseye!" He exclaimed.

The first round hit Mr. Rodansky right between the eyes.

10 the atrium

There was an awkward silence as Nurse Graves wheeled Jeremy down the long white antiseptic hallway towards the elevator doors. The buzzing fluorescent lights hanging from the ceiling above cast an eerie green glow onto the tiled walls and flour. As they approached the elevator, Jeremy could see his funhouse, clown-like reflection in the highly-polished steel of the elevator doors. Nurse Graves brought the wheel chair to rest and selected the button to take the elevator up. He was stunned as he observed his zombie like reflection. His hair was a rat's nest of knots. His eyes, dull and lifeless and surrounded by dark circles appeared like charcoal briquettes resting below his brown. After they entered the elevator Jeremy joked,

"You're giving me the silent treatment and I have only known you for a day. That's a record."

She did not respond.

"Ok. I know why you're not talking to me. I look like shit. You don't go for the unbathed crazy type, do you? You just wait. I'll clean up fine. Once you see me after a good hot shower, a shave and I step into my polo shirt and khaki's you won't be able to keep your hands off of me."

The doors to the elevators opened and she wheeled him into the elevator and selected R for the roof. She replied,

"Mr. Grant, you have a wonderful economy with words. You must have women knocking at your door all day and night with lines like that."

With a sneer and a snicker, he replied,

"You bet I do. I just won't let them out."

The elevator came to rest at the top floor of the hospital. Nurse Graves removed her security badge and swiped it over an electronic eye resting above the key pad of buttons and the doors opened.

She pushed the chair out of the elevator into huge white 85-foot-high rotunda with polished white marble walls. It was topped by a dome lined with green stained-glass windows in the style of Tiffany. At the center of the rotunda was a quiet waterfall cascading over a several boulders made from concrete. Tropical plants and foliage grew along-side the waterfall which fed into a small stream made from white pebbles. Three rows of white park benches circled the water fall.

Male patients dressed in white hospital gowns and slippers mulled about the room. Some were sitting reading books. Others were walking around the waterfall in a counter clockwise motion.

Two patients sitting speaking to each other while sitting on one of the benches stopped their conversation and turned to observe nurse Graves wheel Jeremy across the floor of the rotunda towards a bench. The other patients didn't seem to notice their entry into the room.

The nurses station, staffed with four male nurses, was behind a large glass window located on the far side of the rotunda. Three open rooms spaced ninety feet from each other contained couches, arm chairs and a television set.

Tranquil flute music/sitar music played through the house P.A. system.

Jeremy, noticing that there were no women in the room said,

"There are only dudes in here. Where are all the broads?"

"Broads? Mr. Grant, if what you mean by a broad is women or ladies, our female patients are in the south atrium at the other end of the building. We are in the north wing of the building where our male patients go to collect their thoughts, meet with staff or clergy."

"Ok. I see. So, you wheeled me in hear so I can stare at all of these lunatics while I reflect on what a lousy life and job I have?"

"No. Mr. Grant. You can think about what you want to think about. I suggest you stop feeling sorry for yourself and focus on something other what clever things you can think of saying to me. One of our onsite counselors will be joining you in a few minutes to discuss how you're feeling. Just be patient. Maybe you'll meet a few nice people while you're waiting."

Nurse Graves abruptly turned, walked to the elevators and disappeared behind their mirrored doors. Jeremy sat in silence for several minutes observing his distorted funhouse reflection in the elevator doors. After accepting that he looked like a demented clown wearing a hospital gown, he turned his attention to several patients mulling about on the other side of the room. A clean shaven, slender middle-aged man with shoulder length grey and round wire-rim glasses with blue tinted lenses was playing air guitar without any music. He jumped in the air while swinging his right arm in a clockwise circular motion, left arm extended as if fingering the fretboard of a guitar. He sang and shouted, "People try to put us down....ta, ta talking bout my generation."
As he descended to the floor his hospital gown elevated above his waist due to the up draft created by the jump. This gave Jeremy a brief view of the man's genitalia. Jeremy applauded and yelled across the room,

"Well done Mr. Townsend. Are you a fan of The Who?"

The man knelt motionless on the white marble floor with his head bowed for a moment before responding to Jeremy. Without looking up he responded in a thick British accent,

"What's that mate? The Who? Who the fuck do you think I am?"

Jeremy laughed nervously without responding.

The man jumped to his feet and briskly walked towards Jeremy shouting,

"I am a fucking Beatle! Haven't you heard of bloody John Lennon!?"
Jeremy rolled his wheel chair back a few feet to escape the man's advance.

"Well, your singing the wrong song. That's not a Beatle song. It's a song by The Who."

By the time the last words left Jeremy's mouth the man was standing right in front of him. As he pushed his wire framed glass back onto his nose he said,

"Hello mate, John Lennon. Damn glad to meet you. What's your bloody name?"

Jeremy quickly realized that he had made a mistake by interacting with this individual.
Without responding he began to panic. While pivoting his wheel chair to the right he attempted to push himself away but the man swiftly moved behind the chair and grabbed its hand grips and said,

"Where to mate? Would you like to go see me and the boys at The Cavern tonight? Rory Storm and The Hurricanes are opening for us."

Jeremy gripped the arm rests of the chair as the deranged man began to wheel him about the rotunda in a counter clockwise circular path. Increasing his speed until he was running in circles with Jeremy. The wheel chair was headed straight towards a large marbled pillar. Horrified, Jeremy closed his eyes braced for the impact by pushing his feet against the leg rests of the wheel chair. Anticipating the crash, he wondered how bad it was going to hurt when his body the cold marble when from inside one of the conference rooms a man's voice bellowed,

"Mr. Lennon. Stop pushing that man right now or I will cancel your recording contract with Capital Records. Do you understand me?"

He swerved and avoided the pillar by a few inches brought the chair to a complete stop and let go of the handles. As he walked away he said to Jeremy,

Alright mate. You're at The Cavern. Enjoy the show." The man quietly walked away and sat in a chair on the other side of the room. From behind Jeremy heard the same man who was shouting from one of the conference rooms walk up as he exclaimed sincerely,

"Mr. Grant. I am so sorry. That's one of our long-term patients. He thinks he's former and now deceased Beatle, John Lennon. Looks like he was taking you on a magical mystery tour of The Cavern."

Dazed, Jeremy did not respond.

The man stepped in front of Jeremy breaking his vacant gaze and introduced himself,

"Hi Jeremy. I am Dr. Dean Birkhammer. I have been assigned to your case. Let's get you into the conference room where we can talk."

Dr. Birkhammer was a middle-aged man with lonely sunken piercing beady blue eyes. They peered out like lasers from the shadows of his unusually large brow. His face was framed by a large mane of reddish brown hair, beard and go tee which was peppered with grey. His head seemed to be precariously perched upon his shoulders of his six-foot six husky frame without the assistance of a neck. He wore over-sized faded denim jeans, tan Timberland boots and white dress shirt. The outfit was capped off with a tan corduroy sports coat and red bow tie. His ensemble gave him the appearance of a well-educated sasquatch. He reached out to shake Jeremy's hand but Jeremy did not reciprocate. Instead he said,

"Hold on. How do I know you're a doctor? If that guy thinks he's John Lennon then how do I know you just think you're a doctor?"

Dr. Birkhammer laughed as he replied,

"Fair enough. Here's my security badge."

He unclipped his security badge clipped to his belt and handed it to Jeremy."

Jeremy grasped the badge and looked at it for a few moments and said,

"I guess it looks legit. You could have made it on craft day back at the asylum."

Dr. Birkhammer laughed again,

"I assure you, I am a board and state certified psychologist here at Heather Hill. To prove it I know you were admitted for an episode you had at work. Does that help you clarify who I am?"

"I suppose. Not sure how any of the whack jobs in here would know that."

"Exactly. Now let's wheel you into the conference room and so I can gather some information."

Dr. Birkhammer slowly rotated the wheel chair clock wise and rolled Jeremy into the conference room.

11 the analysis

Dr. Birkhammer gently rolled Jeremy over to a long overstuffed black leather couch sitting against the far wall of the conference room. After locking the wheels of the chair, he invited Jeremy to sit on the couch,

"Jeremy, why don't you go ahead and sit on the couch. Please make yourself comfortable."

The doctor supported Jeremy's arms as he lifted himself up from the chair and onto the couch. After sitting down, he sat back, resting his head on the pillow back of the sofa. Blankly staring at the ceiling, he said,

"So, if this isn't stereotypical I don't know what is."

As Dr. Berkhammer closed the door to the room he seated himself in a matching overstuffed black leather arm chair and asked quizzically,

"What do you mean? You on the comfy couch and me in the arm chair?"

"Yeah. I have never been to a shrink before. It's just like in the movies."

"I suppose. How are you feeling today?"

"My head is pounding. I feel a little dizzy. Other than feeling a little disoriented I feel pretty good."

"Jeremy, what do you remember about your last day at work?"

Jeremy continued to stare at the ceiling. His eyes moved back and forth as if he was searching for the answers written somewhere in tiles of the white drop ceiling.

71

"Doc, all I remember is, Christine, my supervisor, told me they were going to lay me off in a few weeks. I remember going back to my desk and logging into my phone. The next thing I remember is waking up here."

"Alright. What do you do for a living?"

"I am a customer service representative in the call center for Midland Bank in Akron."

Dr. Berkhammer shifted in his seat as he replied,
"Call centers are an extremely stressful environment. Believe it or not I have a variety of patients I see on a regular basis who work in call centers. Most of their ailments stem from their work environment."

"I believe it. It's an awful job. The customers scream at you. The supervisors are constantly on you back. There's little or no hope of advancement. It's the epitome of a dead-end job."

"Not to shock you but to help you with the details regarding your episode at work yesterday."

"Ok"

Doctor Birkhammer opened a spiral bound note book that had been sitting in his lap and began to read off the event as it was dictated to him by the police and paramedics,
"Apparently, you were in the middle of a call with a customer when you began shouting. You ran from your desk and locked yourself in the handicapped stall in the men's room. When the police and paramedics arrived, you begged them not to arrest you. Do you remember any of this?"

"No. Nothing."

"Why do you suppose you thought they were going to arrest you?"

"No idea. I guess for making such a huge scene at work. I don't know."

"What else do you have going on in your everyday life that may have contributed to this outburst and breakdown?"

Jeremy slowly rolled his head to the side so he could look out the tall rectangular windows of the conference room. Staring blankly at the flannel grey skies outside the building his eyes began to fill with tears as he poured out his heart,

"Doc, my life is miserable. I have no life. No family. The loneliness burns holes in my mind. Both my parents have been gone for close to thirty years. My friends, well, you know about friends. Both of my best friends ran off and got married leaving me in the god forsaken shit hole of a town. I haven't heard from any of them since.

My job in the call center is all I have. It's the only time I interact with people. The people I get to interact with are awful. The customers are sniveling, conniving bastards. Management are very similar to Nazi storm troopers. They're just a sadistic bunch of lunatics. Once I am done with my shift I go home to my cat, Camelot, and an empty apartment. It's just me and juice box of wine."

"Your juice box of wine?" The doctor asked.

"Yeah. It's my box of Chardonnay wine that I buy at the grocery store. I have been contemplating finding a way to stick a straw into it so I can drink from it like a juice box. Anyway, I drink myself to sleep. The next day I get up and do it all over again. Now in a few weeks my job is gone."

Doctor Birkhammer cleared his throat as he interjected,
"The holidays are always a hard time of the year to lose a job. It's very tough. It sounds to me like things just got to be too much to take and you had an episode. How about other family. Do you have any brothers and sisters?"

"Are you kidding? I have two brothers and a sister but I consider myself an only child."

"Are you the youngest?"

"How did you guess?"
"Many of the youngest siblings have issues with feeling of inadequacy and abandonment. You say you feel abandoned by your friends and your family. You lead me to believe that you're extremely lonely. Have you considered joining any support groups or joining a club?"

Jeremy shot Dr. Birkhammer a stern look as he replied,

"Oh, come on! Are you fucking kidding me? A support group like Codependence Anonymous or some bullshit like that?"

"Sure, why not?"

Jeremy sat forward and looked directly at the doctor and said,

"I have been to Codependence Anonymous and Adult Children of Alcoholics and it's just a bunch of grown men and women whining and complaining about their parents and their childhood or they drone on and on about some ex-girlfriend or boyfriend who recently broke their hearts. Give me a fucking break."

"So, your parents were alcoholics?"

Jeremy paused, then slowly laid back into the soft overstuffed pillows behind him and closed his eyes.

"Yeah. They were both miserable drunks. It got so bad we were homeless for a short period of time. We never had any food but they always had their booze and cigarettes. Now I am a miserable drunk just like them. At least I can hold down a job."

Doctor Birkhammer casually look at his watch and said,

"Look. There's a lot going on in your mind and in your heart and we are going to need more time to discuss everything. It's getting late. Let's get you back to your room for some rest. I am going to recommend that you stay for at least another night. After that I'd like you to continue to see you at my practice for additional counseling. Ok?"

Jeremy opened his eyes and stared blankly at the ceiling. He asked,

"Do you think I am crazy doc?"

"No. I think you've been through a lot as a kid and it is effecting how you react to situations in your adult life. I believe if you and I work at it we can get your life onto a better track."

"Together? You've got to be kidding me. How much is this togetherness going to cost me?"

"Well, your records indicate that Midland Bank provides you some very good health insurance. So, eighty percent of our sessions and most of your stay here in the hospital is covered. Let's get you back to your room for some rest."

"Ok. You're the boss. It would be nice to get some sleep."

The doctor shifted in his seat and crossed his arms as he asked,
"Jeremy, have you ever thought of hurting yourself or anyone else?"

Jeremy stared blankly past the doctor for several moment before he answered,

"Doc, I am pretty miserable but I would never hurt myself or anyone else. I just want to be happy again."

Uncrossing his arms Doctor Birkhammer responded,
"Just to make sure your out of the woods
I want to keep you hear for another night for observations."

Reaching into his pocket of his sports coat and withdrew a zip lock baggie containing Jeremy's wallet, cell phone and security badge for work.

"Before you go here is your wallet, phone and security badge. The emergency room staff took them from you when you were admitted and I wanted to make sure we returned them to you."

Jeremy took the baggy from the doctor's hand and slid it into the pocket of this white linen bathrobe.

"Thanks doc. I appreciate that."

Doctor Birkhammer called the nurses station and requested someone to assist Jeremy to his room.

12 mr. rodansky

It was 9:00PM. Mr. Rodansky, unshaven with long greasy black hair, was in a beer induced coma struggling to stay awake as he reclined in his green vinyl Lazy Boy recliner while watching Sports Center on his television. The only available light in his living room emanated from the T.V. A Marlboro Red dangling from his lips had burned all the way down to its filter leaving a trail of ashes that tumbled down his Harley Davidson t-shirt and came to rest in a pile on his massive beer belly. A Red and green tattoo of a cobra snake covered each fore arm. They seemed to be alive as they a bathed in the pulsating glow of the television screen and dripping with his perspiration.

The doorbell rang as he reached to his right for his bottle of beer resting on the flimsy plastic T.V. tray table next to his chair causing his thick and bristly hand to flinch knocking the beer bottle off the table and onto the floor. The bottle bounced once on green shag carpet below and came to rest on its side. White Foam poured from the bottle like ejaculate saturating the carpet with beer. Mr. Rodansky spit out his cigarette and bellowed,

"Fucking god damn it! Who's at the freaking door at ten-o-clock at night?"

The doorbell rang again.

The room was spinning as he struggled in his drunken stupor to release himself from the recliner. It seemed to be sucking him in like quick sand so he rolled out of the chair and fell onto the floor knocking the TV table over. Struggling to his feet he shouted,

"Hold on! Just hold the fuck on, will you? I am coming."

As flung the door open his massive six-foot-eight, 240-pound figure filled the door frame. Infuriated, he tactlessly shouted,

"What the fuck do you want son? Go the fuck away. This ain't Halloween you freak."

Standing in front of him on his front porch was a stranger dressed in a black hoodie. The hood was pulled over his head and his face was covered with a demented rubber demon like Halloween mask. The mask was molded with pointed white horns protruding from the forehead. The mouth, open, twisted and contorted and feigning white snake like fangs, had crimson red lips.

"Son? You fucking hillbilly. I am not your son."

Bewildered by the response Mr. Rodansky stepped back to slam the door and yelled,

"Son? Go fuck yourself!"

Before Mr. Rodansky could slam the door, the stranger swiftly moved his right hand under his hoodie and into his pants and pulled out a 357 Magnum from his waste-band. Quickly moving into a power stance to steady his aim he guided the barrel of his weapon towards the center of Mr. Rodansky's forehead and pulled the trigger.

A small red dot appeared above the bridge of his nose. A red spray shot out the back of his head. The bullet blew a softball sized hole from the back of his head and crashed through a wall smashing a mirror behind him into pieces.

For a split moment, Mr. Rodansky's eyes looked glassy and empty. Mouth agape he surprisingly fell straight forward with his face awkwardly pressed against the screen door. As his face slid downward towards the bottom of the door frame the bloody wound left a horrific red streak on the netting of the screen. His massive body crumpled beneath him onto the floor. With his face pressed against the bottom of the screen door a stream of blood flowed from both the entry and exit wounds puddling on the floor just beneath his chin on the kick plate of the door.

The assailant pulled out a small blank white business card from his pants pocket of his jeans and slid it into the lower right corner of the frame of the screen door. Calmly and quietly he slid his weapon back in his waist band, turned and walked down the steps of Mr. Rodansky's front porch and faded into the night. Hand printed on the card he left behind was the phrase, "Press One for Murder".

13 back in his hospital room

The orderlies wheeled Jeremy into his room, locked the wheels of the chair and assisted Jeremy back into his bed. After saying goodnight, he left the room. Jeremy pulled the baggy out of his pocket as he reached for the remote to the television and turned it on. Just as he started to open the baggy his cell phone started to ring. He quickly removed the phone. The call was coming from an unknown number. He answered the phone.

"Hello?"

"Hey there. You still in the nuthouse?"

"Drake?"
"You bet your sorry ass. Have you seen the news yet?"

"Oh, my God! Did Midland leak my story to the press that I cracked up at work?"

"No. Turn to channel three. The story is on right now. Do you remember that customer, Mr. Rodansky, who would call in almost every day and drive us bat shit crazy? Well, someone shot him. He's dead."

Jeremy switched to channel three. Sitting in stunned silence he stared at the television as the on the scene reporter, Hillary Disdain, described the scene,

"This is Hillary Disdain.
I am here on the near east side of Akron where the body of local resident, Jako Rodansky, was discovered by a neighbor who had stopped by Mr. Rodansky's home to bring him his morning paper. Police aren't saying much but it appears that he was murdered in his home by an unknown assailant."

"Jeremy? Are you still there?"

With his gaze transfixed to the television screen Jeremy responded,

"Yes, I am here. Someone beat me to it. Someone actually-killed that fucking bastard? That guy was the biggest dick to me on the phone. He was dick to all of us. He would call and call and call. I have to admit, I often fantasized about taking that fucker out myself."

From the other end of the phone Jeremy could hear Drakes signature high pitched laugh,

"Dude. I know. Almost everyone on our team has spoken to that guy. I am glad to hear your voice. How are you doing? Do they have you in a rubber room?"

With his gaze still transfixed on the television screen he replied,
"It's good to hear from you. Thanks for calling. No. I have a private room. My nurse is pretty hot. The shrink says he doesn't think I am crazy. He thinks I have just been through a lot. I should be out after a few days of observation but I am thinking of checking myself out of this nut house."

"When you get out give me a call. We need to talk."

"Sure. I hope to be back to work when I get out. They can't can me for cracking up or I'll sue their asses."

Drake laughed as he said,

"You'll own that place if they mess with you."

Jeremy chuckled,

"True. Hey! In the news story about Mr. Rodansky the reporter didn't say that he was shot to death. How did you know Mr. Rodansky was shot?

Drake laughed again as he said,
"You are paranoid and crazy aren't' you? I just know someone who lives in the neighborhood.

14 The investigation

At the fourth district police precinct, Captain Tarmelli was reading the report about the victim found in the dumpster at the The Maple House apartments. Tyron Shindles was a seventy-two-year old homeless African American male and veteran of the Vietnam war. He made his way as a small-time drug dealer. People on the street new him as "Little Man" He had a single bullet wound to the back of the head. Nothing else tied the gentleman to the scene. No shell casings were found at the scene. Both victims were shot once with larger caliber bullet, possibly a .357.

Tarmelli said to himself,
"He must have been going through the trash or just finished a drug deal before getting shot. It looks like he was in the wrong place at the wrong time.

His phone rang. Tarmelli answered,

"Fourth Precinct. Tarmelli."

"This is Sergeant Jamerson with forensics. Chief, we have all the evidence from The Maple House shooting ready for you at the warehouse. If you want to come down now I'll show you what we have."

"Sounds good. I'll be down in ten minutes."

After hanging up the phone he grabbed his tweed sports jacket and walked from his desk to the elevator in the hallway.

He stretched a pair of blue latex gloves over his hands. He was in a large warehouse sifting through material from dumpster where Ms. Shanower and Tyron Shindles body was found. The crime scene investigators had tagged and left orderly piles on wooden folding tables and on the floor. Many of items were found in the trash bags that Ms. Shanower had left behind. There were also many items of interest that they had found in her apartment. One item was a spiral bound notebook containing a daily journal.

Tarmelli picked up the journal and sat down to look through it. He was hoping he could find something leading him to the murdered. Maybe there was an ex-lover who had been harassing or stalking her. As he thumbed through the pages he found an entry from September 17 that read,

"Found out my bank account was overdrawn for the third straight month in a row. Called into the call center and for some reason I always get the same asshole representative, Jeremy. Today he insulted me for spending money I did not have while I was eating at Burger King. He said I was dumb as a box of rocks and if I didn't learn how to add and subtract he was going to come over to my apartment and slap some sense into me. I was scared but furious at the same time. Asked for his supervisor and he hung up on me. Called back in and got a representative names Drake. He was just as bad. He hung up on me too. Went to the branch to complain and the branch manager said there she was not aware of Jeremy or Drake. She said she did not have any authority over the representatives that work in the call center. Thank God, I recorded

our conversations. Otherwise, no one would have believed I was treated so rudely."

Tarmelli walked over the end of the table to look at a pile of papers marked, Bank Statements. Forensics found them in the trash bags found at the scene. He picked up the statement on the top of the stack.

Her September bank statement showed that she was overdrawn on her about my $350.00. There were hand written notes scribbled in pen on the first page. One note read,
"5:46PM October 23. Jeremy, Asshole from the call center. Called me a bitch and hung up on me."
On her October statement she wrote,

"November 18, Jeremy, Asshole from call center. Said I was a dumb ass. Hung up on me."

"November 20, Drake, laughed at me when I cried over having my debit card shut off. I hung up on him."

Tarmelli turned his attention to a black cassette tape sitting next to the bank statement. Scribble on the label for side A in blue ink were the words.

Midland Bank Conversations Friday November 18 7:00PM

Tarmelli muttered under his breath,

"Damn. People still use cassette recorders?"

He picked up the cassette and walked it over to a work bench at the back of the warehouse. Sitting on a shelf above the bench was a black Tascam Professional Cassette Deck. He turned on the machine, pressed the eject button which opened the door to the cassette player and slid the cassette in, closed the door and hit play.

After a moment or two Tarmelli heard the recorded sound of a phone ringing. The he heard the voice of an auto attendant giving a greeting and giving the caller options to press on their keypad for service,

"Thank you for calling Midland Bank. Please select from the following.

Press one for Customer Service.

Press two for Lending.

Press 3..."

Before the auto attendant could continue Tarmelli heard a pulse tone from the key selection that what he believed to be Ms. Shanower, made.

There was a brief burst of on hold music then a male customer service representative answered the phone,

"Thank you for calling Midland Bank. This is Jeremy. May I have your name and account number please?"

A woman responded,

"Hi Jeremy. This is Carol Shanower. My account number is 8459253.

Jeremy responded,

"Thank you Ms. Shanower. What is the password on the account.

"My password is "garbage man"."

"Thanks Ms. Shanower. That's correct. How may I help you today?"

"Well, Jeremy. I have a question on my bill."

"On your bill ma'am?"

"Yes, you know, the printout that your bank mails to me every month?"

"Oh sure. You mean your bank statement. Sure. I can help you with that."

"No, you're not listening to me Jeremy I have a question on my bill. There are at least three hundred dollars' worth of fees on my bill and I want to know why."

"Ms. Shanower. That's fine. I am glad to help you. Let me take a look at your account so I can determine what the fees are for. While I am looking let me ask, how did you come up with a password of garbage man?"

"Ms. Shanower, giggled and exclaimed,

"It's a funny story really. I have had some hard times financially and I refuse to pay for the city to pick up my garbage. It costs me $75 a month and I believe it's highway robbery. So, every Friday night I take all my garbage down to the local section eight apartment housing, the Maple House Apartments and dump my garbage in their dumpster. It saves me some money."

Jeremy rolled his eyes as he replied,

"Ok. I guess. That's an interesting way to save. As I look at your account it looks like you have overdraft fees on your account. It looks like you are overdrawn by three hundred dollars. Each of our overdraft fees is thirty-five dollars and you over drew your account eight times which makes up for two hundred and eighty of your overdraft"

Ms. Shanower cleared her throat as she demanded,

"I want all of those fees waived immediately or I'll come down to your call center and raise a stink with your CEO, Mr. Randal Reed. Do you hear me?"

"Ms. Shanower, I can appreciate your concern. Unfortunately, you have been given all of the courtesy credits you are allowed on an annual basis and I am unable to give you any additional credits."

What Tarmelli thought was ear splitting static emitting from the speakers was a high-pitched scream coming from the mouth of Ms. Shanower. As the scream subsided, there was a precious brief silence coming from her end. Then, abruptly, she began to scream and yell again at the top of her lungs demanding Mr. Reed be put on the phone or she was going to come down to the call center and bring her guns with her. Bellowing into the phone that she knew the banks CEO Randal Meed and she demanded to speak to him now. There was a silence and then Tarmeli heard Jeremy reply with a serious steady tone,

"Ms. Shanower. You do you think it's wise to threaten me or the bank? I ask because right in front of me on my computer screen I have all your personal information. I know where you live. I know where you work. I know where you shop and I am sure if I did a little digging I'd know if you had children and who they were. So, I'd be very, very careful or I may show up unexpectedly one day while you're watching reruns of The Price Is Right."

There was dial tone and the recording ended.

Hastily, Tarmelli picked up his cell phone and called Sergeant Sarah Wickland.

After two rings Wickland answered the phone,

"Sergeant Wickland. Third precinct."

"Hey there Sarah. You know that serial murderer case I have been working on?"

"Sure. The one where the perp leaves the business card with "Press one for murder" written on them."

"That's the one. I have a lead on a potential suspect. I think he works down at the Midland Bank call center off of Midland Court. Let's head down there and see if we can chat with one of the customers service representatives that works there. I'll give them a call ahead of time to see if he's working tonight."

"Ok. Chief. If he's working I'll meet you in the parking lot in fifteen minutes."

"Sounds good. I'll see you in a few.'

Tarmelli hung up dialed 1-800-MIDLAND. After selecting prompt number one a pleasant-sounding young lady on the phone named Tarisha answered the line.

Tarmelli interrupted her introduction,

"Excuse me young lady. I just have a quick question. Does a customer service representative work there by the name of Jeremy?"

The woman replied,

"Um, yes. He sits two rows behind me. He's here tonight. Would you like me to transfer you to him?"

Tarmelli cleared his throat and said,

"No. That's ok. I'll call back. How late does he work tonight?"

"Sir, he's on the same shift me so he'll be here until eleven."

Tarmelli, thanked the young lady and hung up. He texted Sergeant Wickland,

"He's working until eleven. See you in a few minutes."

15 Return to work

Dread filled Jeremy's heart as he parked his car in the parking lot for Midland Bank. He reclined the seat of his car, closed his eyes and desperately searched every wrinkle of his mind for an avenue of escape. There had to be an excuse he could come up with to call in sick for just one more day. But there was no escape. He had already missed a week of work and if he continued to call in sick without an excuse from Doctor Birkhammer his job would be in jeopardy.

Grabbing his plastic grocery bag containing his lunch he exited the car and closed the car door and began his long agonizing walk from the parking lot to his building. In a panic his mind strained to remember all of his passwords he would need to log onto the phones and all the systems to start taking calls.

A cold sweat covered his body as he approached the doors to the lobby of the building. With his heart pounding in his ears he pulled back on the horizontal cold grey steel handle to the door but the door would not open.

He cursed himself out loud,

"God, damn it Jeremy! You stupid fuck! You've got to swipe your security badge to get in the damn building."

He swiped his badge and the door buzzed and entered the main lobby. As he approached the security desk he saw Brandon behind the security desk hunched over his smart phone completely self-absorbed in writing a text message. Jeremy leaned against the desk and pointed his right hand at his head like a gun with his index finger straight out and thump pointed up and said maniacally,

"Stick-em up buddy or I'll blow your head clean off."

Expecting an armed intruder Brandon dropped his phone. It clattered on the tiled floor as he lurched back in his chair only to see Brandon standing there with his finger pointing at him. Brandon exclaimed,

"God, damn you man. If I had my piece on me you'd be in sorry shape my man."
Jeremy laughed as he replied,

"Only fucking with you. It's good to see you again."

Brandon quickly gathered himself and reached across the security wall in front of him and shook Jeremy's hand. With a large welcoming-smile he said,

"Jeremy! It's so good to see you again. How have you been? My friend, you were in sorry shape when they carted you out of here."

Jeremy squeezed Brandon's hand as he replied,

"I was doing fine until I pulled into the parking lot."

"I hear you. I hear you my friend. But we got to do what we got to do to keep food in our bellies."

"True. You get any more reports on crazy customers threatening the call center?"

"A few. We had a wild one while you were gone who said he was going to come up here and shoot the place up. I forwarded his name and address to the authorities. Not sure what they do with the information but we had two Akron police cruisers parked out front the entire time you were gone. So, I am guessing they took it seriously enough to have the police outside."

"No way. Who was the customer?"

Brandon open the Excel spread sheet on his computer where he kept the list of names and addresses of customers who posed potential threats. As his eyes scanned the list he said,

"Let's see here. It was Robert Randolph. Drake took the call. I guess the guy keeps calling trying to get into his mother's account but he's not a signer on the account."

Jeremy eyes widened as he replied,

"God damn. I don't remember much about that night I had my breakdown but I remember Mr. Randolph was the last customer I talked to before I went off my rocker. He calls all the time trying to get into his mother's account."

Brandon shook his head as he said,

"It's takes all kinds. People are desperate these days and will do anything to make a quick buck."

Jeremy stepped back from the security desk as he replied,

"True. Well, Brandon. I better get logged into the phones before they fire my ass."

Brandon reached out his hand again to shake Jeremy's. The two men shook hands and Jeremy turned to go to his desk.

He turned from the security desk and made his way down the long hallway leading to the call center. Making a stop at the break room to drop off his lunch he saw Drake sitting at a table with his back to him, eyes transfixed on his iPhone as he read emails.

The call center breakroom is a place of sanctuary from the phones for many employees. It's where customers service representatives go to escape the pressures of the day by medicating themselves with snack food and coffee. For Many employees, it's a place they can congregate to voice their concerns to one another about how poorly they are treated by management and the customers.

The Midland Bank break room is small sparsely decorated. The buzzing fluorescent lights set into the ceiling cast a greenish glow upon the company's posters of propaganda lining the walls. Each poster was hung in a cheap black plastic frame contained a message of inspiration. One was a 24 inch by 36-inch print with the message printed in bold block letters against a bright yellow background that read, "YOU ARE FIRST CALL RESOLUTION. Another poster of the same size decorating the wall was a color photograph of an athletic woman on a mountain top silhouetted against a setting sun and a bright blue sky. The message beneath her feet written in white lacy scrip read, "Perseverance will get you to the top." An anonymous and apparently disgruntled employee hastily scribbled an opposing message in black magic marker above the woman's head that read, "Bite me you bitch!"

The room contained a small kitchen counter top with a toaster, one small microwave oven and two coffee pots. Next to the counter was a side by side chrome industrial sized refrigerator. Two small round kitchen tables with laminate tops surround by mismatched plastic backed chairs sat in the center of the room. At the far end of the room stood a top loading water cooler. Next to the water cooler was a tall black vending machine containing a variety of junk food snack including jelly filled donuts, beef jerky and the ever-popular selection of salted chips and chocolate bars.

As Jeremy entered the room he stopped and, in an attempt to startle Drake, he shouted,

"Hey Dude. I am out of the nut house."

Drake was not alarmed. He looked up and immediately began to smile. He jumped from his seat, walked over to Jeremy, shook his hand and gave him a big bear hug. He said,

"Oh, my fucking god! Dude. It's so good to have you back. Christine said you were coming back this week. How are you feeling?"

Jeremy laughed as he replied,

"Honestly, I was doing fine until I pulled into the parking lot."

They both laughed. Then Drake asked,

"Do you have a few minutes to talk?"

"Sure. I got here earlier than usual. What's going on?"

They both pulled back a chair at the nearest table and sat down. Drake hung his head as he started to speak.

"Dude. I admire your dedication coming back to work after losing it. Believe it or not, I have come close to losing my mind a couple of times here. This place sucks. Honestly, I am not sure how much more I can take. The customers that call in are awful. Don't get me started on the crappy supervisors. I am thinking of quitting."

Jeremy looking bewildered replied,

"Don't you know?"

"Don't I know what?"

"I guess they didn't tell you. They are closing the call center after the holidays. We're all getting laid off."

Drake pushed himself back into his seat and exclaimed,

"No fucking way dude! That's sucks! Everyone's getting laid off."

"Yep. They are going through with the Christmas party then after the new year the axe is going to fall."

Drake pounded the table with his fist as he said,

"God, dam it. If I had quit then I wouldn't have gotten unemployment."

"That's correct. You would have been shit-out of luck."

"Correct."

Drakes eyes widened as he asked,

"How did you know? Why would they tell you and not the rest of us?"

He shot Drake a sober look out of the corner of his eye as he whispered,

"I have been eating Christine out in the stairwell on my breaks and at lunch. I guess I am so good at hit she convinced upper management to keep me on board. So, she clued me in."

Drake eyes popped wide open as he exclaimed,

"Get the fuck out of here dude! If your tongue got anywhere near that rancid behemoth it would rot and fall out of your mouth."

Jeremy burst out laughing,

"Seriously, I have been here a while and they see how dedicated I am. They were going to keep me on board until after the layoffs. Also, they don't want everyone to just walk out or do something violent after they make the announcement."

Drake lowered his voice and leaned in close to Jeremy as he said,

"Dude. Let's go out to the parking lot. I want to show you something."

Jeremy looked perplexed and said,

"What do you want to show me? I have to be on the phones in fifteen-minutes."

Drake insisted,

"Come on man. Christine knows you had a breakdown because of work. She'll cut you some slack this one time."

"Alright. Make it quick. I really don't need Christine coming down on me right now. Seriously, I don't.

They got up from the table and walked briskly down the hall, past the guard's station and out through the main doors of the building and into the parking lot. They walked to an area at the back of the lot furthest from the front doors of the building. Drake pulled out his cell phone, unlocked it and handed it to Jeremy. He said,

"Look at this."

Jeremy looked down at the cell phone and saw the Drake was logged into the Little Black Book application that he had designed. On the screen in alphabetical order were a list of names. Jeremy looked at the names and saw Mr. Rodansky's name. He asked,

"What is this? I see you have Mr. Rodansky's name. Are the other names customer names too?"

"Yes. Dude. I can't stand these people. I was making a list and going home at night and looking their profiles up on Facebook. Their banking records show me where they live, where they work and how much money they make. Shit I even know the names of their kids and where they go to school."

Jeremy scrolled through the names in complete silence. After a moment or two he looked around the parking lot to make sure no one was watching or close enough to hear his response. He pulled out his phone, unlocked it and pulled up his copy of the Little Black Book. He handed it to Drake and said,

"Take a look."

Drakes mouth hung open in complete surprise as he scrolled through what looked like an identical list of customer names. He said,

"No fucking way. We have practically the same list of names. So, you think these people suck as much as I do. I see you call Mr. Rodansky, "Fucktard Rodansky"."

Jeremy laughed as he replied,

"Yeah. When I saw that he was murdered I wasn't surprised at all. I was actually a little happy about it. Don't you fucking dare tell anyone I told you that."

Drake furrowed his brow as he replied,

"No fucking way. I wouldn't tell anyone. That guy was nuts."

"He sure was."

Drake nervously looked around the parking lot as he asked,

"Have you ever thought of just showing up at one of the fucker's homes? You know, go to one of these dickhead customer's homes and going postal on them?"

Jeremy stepped back and asked,

"Why do you ask? Did you kill Rodansky?"

"No. I swear. When I saw it on the news I was yelling, "Someone beat me to it!""

"How did you know he got shot. They still haven't said anything about how he died on the news?"

"I told you. I know someone who lives in his neighborhood. Let's have a few beers tonight at The Squeaky Wheel after work to talk about it."

Jeremy's voice cracked as he replied,

"Dude, I just got out of the hospital. I don't need any trouble."

Drake touched Jeremy on the shoulder and said,

"There's nothing to worry about. Trust me."

"Ok. I better get back inside and log onto the phones."

They turned and walked from the parking lot into the lobby of the building. As they approached Brandon at the security desk they saw a man and woman speaking to him. Brandon called over to Jeremy,

"Hey Jeremy. Someone is here to see you."

Jeremy looking concerned walked over to the security desk and asked,

"Someone wants to see me?"

"Yes, we have Captain Tarmelli and Sergeant Wickland from the Akron police department that want to ask you a few questions. I 'll let Christine know you won't be on the phones for a few minutes."

Detectives Tarmelli and Wickland turned and faced Jeremy. Tarmelli asked,

"Are you Jeremy Gant?"

The palms of Jeremy's hands turned sweaty and his heart began to race as he responded,

"Um, yes. What's going on?"

Both showed Jeremy their badges as they responded,

"Mr. Gant, I am Captain Tarmelli and this is my partner Sergeant Wickland. We want to ask you a few questions about one of your customers."

Jeremy looked at Brandon and said,

"Do you know if there is a board room we could meet in?"

Brandon replied,

"There is the interview room. It's open right now."

Jeremy replied,

"Let's use the interview room right here off the lobby."

He then led Tarmelli and Wickland to the interview room. Once inside Jeremy turned on the overhead fluorescent lights and they flickered to life After closing the door they each sat down at a small rectangular table. Tarmelli sat across the table from Jeremy and Wickland sat next to Jeremy.

Tarmelli inquired,

"Jeremy, do you recall ever speaking to a Ms. Shanower, Carol Shanower on the phones?"

Jeremy looked at Tarmelli and then at Wickland. His voice trembled as he spoke,

"Um, well. The name Wickland sounds familiar. We have a Ms. Shanower that calls in repeatedly asking for overdraft fees to be credited to her account. She's well known. I'll bet everyone here in our call center has had conversations with her. They usually escalate to the point where she demands to speak to our CEO Randy Reed. Why do you ask?"

"Well, Jeremy. A few nights ago, Ms. Shanower was murdered. After going through the evidence related to her murder you name came up. We found records that she kept detailing phone conversations that she had with Midland about the accounts she held here. In one specific conversation, she referred to you specifically. Even more she made an audio recording of that conversation. In that recording after she demanded to speak to Mr. Reed , you suggested that you might show up at her house. "

Jeremy's hands trembled as he placed them both over his face and hung his head. His voice quivered as he spoke,

"Oh, my God! She recorded that conversation and now she is dead. You guys think I had something to do with her death?"

Sergeant Wickland responded dryly,

"That's correct. Where were you on the evening of Friday, November 18th?"

Jeremy threw his head back and his eyes looked towards the ceiling as if the answer was in the green glow of the fluorescent lights. He replied,

"Friday. I work every Friday until 11pm."

"Who is your supervisor. We would like to verify your schedule with her."

"Christine, Christine Cronk. She's here tonight and probably wondering where I am. It's my first day back to work. I was in the hospital for a week."

Wickland responded with concern,

"I am sorry to hear that. What was wrong?"

Jeremy reached behind his head and rubbed the back of his neck as he responded,

"Well, this job can really get to you. I kind of lost it one night and I had a breakdown. The doc says it was a nervous breakdown. So, they kept me over at Heather Hill for a few days for observations."

Wickland responded,

"I am sorry to hear that. I hope you're feeling better. I am sorry you haven't been feeling well but on the recording, we heard you insinuate that you were going to go to Ms. Shanower's home. Did you ever go to her house or physically threaten her?"

"Jeremy, as if in a panic, quickly leaned forward and proclaimed,

"No! Never! That lady was a lunatic. I would say things just to get her off the phone. All of us did. She would call in over and over again trying to get her fees waived. One day she talked to thirty different reps in our call center. I would never harm anyone.

Damn! She threatened several of us. We reported her to Brandon. He's the security guard that works during my shift."

Tarmelli responded,

"How do you report it to him?"

"We have to fill out a report. It's hand written form documenting the details of the call. You know, the date, time, account numbers and who we spoke with. We also give a brief description of the potential threat."

Tarmelli fidgeted in his chair and asked,

"What does Brandon do with these reports?"

"He keeps them in a folder at the front desk in our lobby. He gives a copy of each report to Mr. Reed. Then he calls the local police to let them know that they have had several threats."

Tarmelli looked at detective Wickland and said,

"Let's contact the local precinct and get copies of the reports from the dispatch office so we can see the details of the threats."

"Will do chief. There might be some correlation between that list and who our victims have been."

Jeremy rubbed his forehead as he remembered,

"The cops were here for a couple of weeks parked out front. They had two cruisers parked in front of the lobby doors. Brandon wouldn't tell us why but they were there every day for over two weeks."

Tarmelli responded,

"There will definitely be a record of that at the precinct. Thanks for letting me know. We will look into it. Jeremy, thanks for talking with us. We'll be in touch if we need anything else."

Jeremy sat up straight. In a worried voice he asked,

"That's it? You come in here to see if I murdered someone and all I get is "Thanks for talking with us"? Come on officers. You don't believe me, do you?"

Taremelli replied,

"We're going to check with your supervisor to see if you were in fact, at work on that evening. If that checks out you're in the clear for now."

Jeremy replied,

"Well, I was."

Tarmelli and Wickland stood up and said to Jeremy,

"Tell you what, just sit tight in here while we speak to Christine. If everything checks out we'll say goodnight."

"Ok."

Tarmelli and Wickland stood up from their chairs left the room closing the door behind them.

Jeremy closed his eyes, leaned forward and laid his head on the table. As if protecting himself from falling debris he covered the back of his head with his arms and let out a loud sigh of despair. He couldn't think clearly as his thoughts were in a tangle. He groaned out loud as he thought of all the mistakes and questions. He thought of all the customers he had said threatening things to over the years. Did they have recordings of him too he asked himself? What if the police take him to jail. What if Christine doesn't have a record of him being at work that night? It seemed to be an eternity before he heard the interview room door click open. Tarmelli Wickland came back in the room.

Jeremy sat up in his chair as Tarmelli spoke,

"Well, Mr. Gant. You're in the clear for now. Your supervisor has you here until 11:15PM that night. So, you're in the clear for now. Don't leave town. We'll be in touch. Here's my card. If you know of anyone on your staff who would have wanted to do harm to Ms. Shanower please give me a call."

Jeremy's eye's opened wide as he responded,

"Oh, thank God! Yes, I will call you."

Tarmelli responded,

"Ok, Mr. Gant. You have a good night."

Jeremy did not respond as the two detectives walked out.

Christine appeared in the doorway and said,

"Hey there. We need to talk."

16 THE SQUEAKY WHEEL

The Squeaky Wheel was a hole in the wall near the campus of
Akron University where Drake worked weekends as a bartender.
It was the only place near campus where they didn't water down
the booze.

Jeremy always referred to it as an "old man bar" because it's
regulars were mostly Vietnam War vets hunched over their beer

and whisky. He couldn't remember the last time an attractive woman walked through the doors.

It had been a local watering hole over the last fifty years. Its walls plastered with one dollar bills that patrons donated with each visit. Each dollar bill is signed by the customer along with the date of their visit. No one remembers how or when the tradition got started but visitors have kept it going throughout the years.

As Jeremy and Drake walked in they took up residence in their favorite booth at the back of the bar near an antique juke box. Jimmy, who looked more like an old prospector than a bar tender, called over to Drake and Jeremy,

"You guys having the same, pitcher of Wilken Lite?"

Drake responded sarcastically,

"Aye, aye, captain. Get us each a shot of J.D. too if you don't mind."

Drake leans forward with his elbows on the table. With an excited look in his eyes he says,

"Jeremy. Look. You know how bad most of our customers are. They are the biggest fuckers in the world. I am not sorry but when I heard about Mr. Rodansky I was thrilled. This guy had it coming."

Just then Jimmy the bartender brought them two glasses and a pitcher of Wilkens Lite beer. He produced two shot glasses with

Squeaky Wheel etched in the glass from his apron and said, "Hold on fellas. I'll be right back with your whiskey."

Jeremy wrung his hands as he responded while Drake poured them each a beer,

"Drake, listen. I know. Our customers suck. But I think I am in trouble. It's really-bad and I am fucking freaking out. The cops stopped by the call center today to ask me some question about one of our customers. Ms. Shanower? That crazy lady who called in thirty times in one day to get overdraft fees waived? The cops told me she's dead. She was murdered and they found a tape recording that she made of me talking to her on the phone when she called in to our call center. I am on the recording telling her I was going to show up at her house. Can you believe this? Oh, my fucking God they think I killed her!"

Drake pushed himself back against his seat and said,

"No fucking way. You're fucking with me, aren't you?"

Jeremy shoved himself back into his seat and threw his arms out to his sides as he exclaimed loudly,

"No! I am not fucking kidding. Two homicide detectives showed up and took me into the interview room to see where I was the night she was murdered."

"Ok. Ok. Calm down. If they thought you were the killer then why didn't they arrest you right on the spot?"

"They Checked with Christine and my time card shows I was here until eleven fifteen that evening taking calls. So, they cleared me, for now they say, of being a suspect. Assholes told me not to leave town. When they left, they said they would be in touch. Man, if the pressures of work sent me to the nuthouse this is going to have me back there sooner than later."

Drake covered his face with both hands,

"That's fucked up. Oh, my God. We have her name in our little black book. At least I do. That bitch was fucking crazy. She actually recorded one of the conversations when she called in and it just happened to be the exact moment she spoke to you?"

"Yes! I heard it for myself."

Drake laughed nervously as he replied,

"Wow! And I thought we were safe being smart asses over the phone because the bank is too God damn cheap to invest in the software to record our calls."

"I know. I know. I never thought that any of our customers would be smart enough to record one of our conversations."

A twisted grin appeared on Drakes face as he said,

Hey! Someone is knocking off our customers. She's the second one to get murdered."

"I must admit, there were times when I wanted to go to different customer's homes and put a bullet through their thick skulls but I never attempted it."

Jimmy returned to their table and interrupted them to pour each of them a shot. He winked and walked back behind the bar.

Drake picked up his shot glass and raised it and said,

"A toast to our customers demise."

Jeremy's paused and looked at the shimmery golden liquid in the shot glass for several moments. His hand trembled as he raised his glass and said dispassionately, ,

"To our customers demise."

As if the shot glasses and its contents before them were rare and precious jewels, both men calmly and carefully brought their shot glass to their lips to ensure not a single drop was wasted. In an abrupt motion, they each opened their mouths and threw back the bourbon. After a deep hard swallow their eyes teared up as the whiskey slowly burned its way down and into their stomachs.

After Wiping his mouth Drake said,

"Dude. Don't worry. You were at work and Christine backed you up. You're in the clear."

"I know. But what if they just stick it on me just to close the case? It happens all the time on those cop shows on television."

"That's television. Sure, that can happen in real life but it would never stand up in court. Dude, once again, you were at work the night she died. Hey! I didn't know you were a programmer. How long did it take you to design the Little Black Book application?"

Jeremy still recovering from his shot of whiskey winced as he replied,

"Well, it took me a while. At least a year of design and working on prototypes. The hard part was getting it to disappear from screen of the phone and figuring out how to allow the user to reopen it. Once I got that figured out it was a piece of cake."

"It's an awesome app. If the heat is one maybe we should delete the app from each of our phones. If the cops get a warrant and find the app with all the customers names listed we're going to be in deep, deep, shit. At least you are."

"Drake! Stop! You just got through telling me I am in the clear and now you're saying we should delete the app just in case. I am going to delete mine tonight. I have the address book back up at home on an external hard drive. Do you have yours back up?"

"It never occurred to me to back it up. I will tonight."

Drake leaned forward, took a sip of beer and asked,

"What do you think of our CEO Mr. Reed?"

Jeremy replied sharply,

"He's a prick. The epitome of a corporate sociopath. He runs that place like a prison. If anyone should get killed it's that guy."

Drake laughed as he said sarcastically,

"Ok dude. Tell me how you really feel."

Jeremy's mood quickly became even more somber as he discussed his distaste,

"This guy has the audacity to pay next to nothing for an hourly wage while he goes sailing on his yacht to the Bahama's to go golfing and come back to the office and brag about his exotic trip. Then, behind closed doors, he decides to shut down the call center. The son of a bitch is shutting it down near the holidays too. What kind of sadistic prick chooses the holidays to shut down a call center?"

Drake pushed himself away from and said,

"We should do something to him at the Christmas Party."

"Like what?"

Drake took a large gulp of beer and said,

"You know how I have that old Chevy conversion van that I converted into a portable D.J. booth? The one I use to D.J. and sometimes bartend from?"

"Sure. What about it?"

'Mr. Reed asked me to tend bar at this year's Christmas party. What if this year I slipped something into that fucker's drink? Then we take him out back, put him in the van and drive him somewhere outside of Columbus. We'll let him loose in the middle of nowhere and see if the he can find his way home like some dogs do when they are lost. Or, we'll send him snipe hunting."

Jeremy laughed,

"Dude that would be hilarious but then what? We better not do anything. Especially now that the cops are considering me as a suspect."

Drake looking perplexed replied,

"Ok. Let's just slip something into his drink before he gets on stage to do his Christmas skit. Those Christmas skits are fucking lame. You know they are. How fucking entertaining would it be to see him making a fool out of himself as he stumbled around on stage, slurring his speech. Maybe he'd even fall off and break his neck."

"Where are you going to get the drugs?"

"Remember? My mom is a nurse. We have all kinds of pills in our medicine cabinet at home. She's hopped up on muscle relaxers all the time because she messed up her back turning some old fat ass over in his bed one day. I'll give him something that will knock him on his ass."

Before Jeremy could answer there was a breaking news bulletin on the television from Channel 3 from **Hillary Disdain,**

"I'm Hillary Disdain and we just got word that there has been another murder here in the Akron metropolitan area. A Mr. Dean Bartlett was found dead in his car at a local park. Apparently, the victim of a single gunshot to the head. Police officials aren't saying too much more but we spoke to Captain Tarmeli of the Akron Police Department and he seems to believe that this murder may be related to the serial killings that have been reported over the last several weeks. We'll have more tonight at eleven."

Jeremy and Drake sat with their eyes transfixed on the television screen hanging from the ceiling. That sat for several seconds before either man said anything.

Jeremy spoke first,

"This can't be happening. Someone is killing our customers one by one. Do you remember Mr. Bartlett?"

With his eyes still glued to the screen watching news video of the crime scene Drake replied,

"Sure. He was the guy that kept calling his bank statement a bill because he kept getting so many overdraft fees. That guy threatened me every time he called. He's in my little black book too. How about yours?"

"Great minds think alike. Yes, he's in there. I reported this guy to our security guard, Brandon, so many times, has an entire notebook on this guy.

17 THE WARRANT

Christmas Eve 4:00PM

As Tarmelli sits on the edge of Detective Wickland's desk, he looks into his half-empty coffee cup. Swirling the cup in a clockwise circular motion several drops of coffee splash onto his snow man adorned Christmas tie. Mindlessly wiping the droplets away with his hand, he says,

"Something just doesn't sit right with me. So, far we have one potential suspect but he has an air tight alibi for that evening. There is no one else even close to being a suspect other than the

Jeremy fella. But there is no way he could have gotten off of work and made it all the way to the Maple House Apartments and Killed Ms. Shanower. Yet, he's is literally on tape insinuating that he is going to come to her house and cause her harm."

Detective Wickland leaned back in her chair and folder her hands behind her head and replied,

"I know. But maybe he just likes to say outrageous things to customers to keep them from calling back in. After all, she wasn't killed at home. She was killed miles from her house at an apartment complex."

"I know. I am going to give Jeremy's supervisor a call and see if she'll let me come back and take a look through his desk to see if there is any evidence linking him to the murders."

"Don't we need a warrant for that?"

"Not if his supervisor gives of the ok to search his desk. It's not technically his property. Anything at his desk is the property of Midland Bank."

Tarmelli pulled out his smart phone and called Christine's cell phone number. After several rings she answered,

Pleasantly Captain Tarmelli said,

"Hi Christine. This is Captain Tarmelli. I would like to come back and ask you a few additional questions. Are you in the office tonight?

Christine cleared her throat as she replied,

"Yes, I am here. I am just cleaning a few loose ends up. Our Christmas party is tonight and we are shutting the phone lines down until after Christmas. How soon will you be here?"

"We will be there in fifteen minutes."

"Ok. That's fine."

"Ok See you in a few minutes. Bye."

Tarmelli ended the call.

After their fifteen-minute drive, they arrive at the call center. Brandon the guard that's traditionally on duty at the front desk is now at the Christmas party. Tyron, his back-up, lets them into the building. Tarmelli informs Tyron that they are there to see Christine. Tyron calls Christine on her phone. After a short wait she appears in the lobby to greet the officers,

"Hello officers. Has something changed? Is Jeremy in trouble?"

Wickland responded,

"No. What we would like to do is take a look at his desk. We want to see if there is anything at his work station that would link him to the murder of your customer, Ms. Shanower. Do you mind taking us to his desk?"

"Yes. I can do that. He is very organized and his desk is immaculate. I just can't believe he would be involved in such an awful thing. It breaks my heart that we have to let him go after the holidays. He's a great worker and a nice guy too or so I thought."

"Thanks Christine. It will only take us a minute or two. Is he working tonight?"

"No. The call center shut down early for the Christmas party. I would imagine he's on the way to the banquet center now."

As they entered call center Tarmelli and Wickland each stretched a pair of blue latex gloves over the hands. Wickland asked Christine,

"Where is his desk?"

Christine pointed towards in the general direction of his desk as she responded,

"It's at the back wall in the center near the large concrete pillar."

Christine escorted Tarmelli and Wickland to Jeremy's desk. She waited at the end of the aisle of desks at the two detectives began their search.

As they approached they noticed that there were no drawers under his desk. There wasn't even a filing cabinet. His desk was very clean. It was unusually sparse. There were no note pads, books or documents anywhere on his desktop. The only visible items were his keyboard and mouse. There wasn't even a filing cabinet.

Tarmelli said dryly,

"Well, it looks like we won't be here very long."

Wickland chuckled,

"No. We should be home in time for dinner."

As Tarmelli leaned over the computer monitor to look behind it his sports coat brushed against the key board on the desk top moving it several inches.

Wickland said in an urgent voice,

"Chief! Look what's under the keyboard."

Tarmelli stood back and looked down at the keyboard. Sticking out from underneath the keyboard were several plain white business cards. He reached down and picked them up and shuffled through each of them. As he flipped them over his eyes opened wide. The hand-written message on the other side of each card read,

"Press one for murder"

Tarmelli stepped back from the desk without moving his gaze from the precious piece of evidence he held in his hand and said,

"I knew it! Call the District Attorney. We need to get an arrest warrant for one Jeremy Gant.

Tarmelli walked over to Christine standing at the end of the aisle and asked,

"Do you know where Jeremy is right now?"

"Sure, he's probably headed to the Christmas party at DiNardo's Party Center. That's where I am headed now."

Tarmelli removed an evidence bag from the side pocket of his sports coat and placed the business cards inside. The two detectives quickly removed their latex gloves, briefly shook Christine's hand and hurriedly walked out of the call center and back to their car.

"Christine. Thanks for your help."

Meekly, Christine replied,

"Sure. No problem."

18 THE CHRISTMAS PARTY

It was 4:30PM. As Local big band favorite, Tommy Jay and The Crooners, started playing an upbeat version of White Christmas A heavy snow had begun to fall outside. Employees shook the snow from their coats as they shuffled in to the DiNardo Party Center lobby. Most of the men came dressed in conservative formal business attire while many of the women dressed garishly. Several of the ladies, especially Trina Dosherman, were sporting leather miniskirts, with platform soul five-inch stiletto shoes topped off by a tight low-cut blouse revealing their cleavage.

The companies Christmas party was always held on Christmas Eve. CEO Randal Reed thought that by having the party the night before Christmas made it more festive and added to the fun. In previous years one third of the employee base turned down the invitation to the party so, this year, he made it mandatory that everyone attend. As an incentive, he stated that no one would get a share of the company's profits if they were truant . This compounded the deep-seated resentment that most employees had for him.

Over the last thirty years, Midland Bank had been utilizing the DiNardo Party Center for its company Christmas party. This was the traditional banquet hall used for weddings, birthday parties, corporate events and high school proms. It had four banquet rooms. Three of them were small one thousand square foot rooms for smaller occasions. Midland always rented the ten thousand square foot Birchwood Room with a huge stage for its Christmas party.

Midland spared no expense when it came to throwing this party. There was always a live band, top of the line catered food and an open bar. Many of the employees who felt that they were underpaid felt that Midland made this such an extravaganza so they could ease their conscience for being so thrifty with the payroll. At last year's party Bill Moyer, a teller from one of the branches, had a few too many Appletinis and stood on his table and yelled at the top of his lungs,

"Pay me shit but give me a huge Christmas party to make up for your cheap ass selves. Let them eat cake. Let them eat cake!"

He then threw his martini glass to the ground where it shattered in pieces. He was quickly subdued by his wife and some friends and convinced to sit down and have some coffee. Many employees felt the same way but did not dare raise their voices at the risk of losing their jobs. Many were single mothers and fathers who were working two jobs to keep food on the table.

This was the big event of the year for the bank. It was especially big for the call center employees. Hoping they could turn the heads of the male dominated upper management, many female employees prepared a slutty ensemble that included five-inch stiletto heels and mini-skirts several months in advance. Often times in the breakroom you would hear women discussing what shoes they would wear or where they would buy their dress. Some saw it as no more than a pitiful version of a high school prom. Others thought it a desperate attempt at pacifying a weary and unhappy employee base who felt that they were underpaid by giving everyone free booze and food. Either way, most people would go and attempt to have a good time.

As in previous years, Chief Executive Officer Randal Reed and Vice President Corey Gandolf were the gregarious hosts for the evening. They would climb on stage and grab the microphone. Like some tawdry Las Vegas act they would tell jokes and roast one another with mildly off-color humor for what seemed like an eternity. It was painful performance to watch. Some made a half-hearted attempt to laugh at their sophomoric charade but most sat in silence as the two men got drunk and stumbled over themselves in attempt to prove to their inferior subordinates that they too were human.

CEO Randal Reed has all the characteristics of psychopath. Many of the employees were shocked by his lack of empathy in previous years when he had layoffs around the holidays. Ms. Shanebacker, a branch manager at one of the bank branches was convinced he was a sadist by letting people go at that time of years. She could be heard on more than one occasion saying,

"He's into cruel and unusual punishment. I hope he gets hit by a gas truck and chokes to death on his own blood."

Randal was a well-kept and handsome man. His brown, lush and finely groomed head of hair and finely trimmed mustache was known to turn more than a few of the lady's heads. Always donning pastel colored, tailor-made fitted shirts with his monogram, R.R, stitched onto the pocket of each shirt emphasized his egocentricity. His every move and word seemed to be carefully choreographed as if he thought he were a character in some Broadway, Shakespearean play. Many of the men within Midland thought he resembled a department store mannequin. There was nothing natural, honest or sincere about this man. He was the epitome of an executive.

Most people headed for the fully stocked bar located just inside the ballroom after they checked their coats to get a drink from Drake. For the last several years, Drake volunteered to be the bartender. His part-time job outside of the bank was as a bartender at The Squeaky Wheel. As the ceremonial bartender for the evening, he was dressed in a red velvet vest over a white dress shirt, green bow tie and black dress pants. The ensemble was completed with an oversized Santa hat with a white ball of fur at its peak lazily drooped behind his head.

As he finished wiping down the bar he spotted Jeremy entering the ballroom with an extremely exotic looking   brunette at his side. Jeremy was wearing his one and only grey business suit and tie. The center of his tie was adorned with a Santa with a huge red nose stitched into the fabric. Beneath Santa it read, "Squeeze me!" His date was of a caliber that Drake had never seen Jeremy associate with. Her wavy brunet hair sensually draped over her shoulders shimmered. She was wearing a diamond studded choker around her neck, black leather low cut min dress with an off-the-shoulder sweetheart neckline. Her long beautiful legs encapsulated by tight black leather thigh high boots with a gold metal five-inch stiletto heel.

As they approached the bar Jeremy said to Drake,

"Hey bartender, would you like to squeeze my Santa?"
Drake laughed and he reached out to squeeze Santa's belly in the middle of Jeremy's tie. After he squeezed a distorted digital recording of Jingle Bells played accompanied by a recording of Santa's voice saying loudly,

"Ho! Ho! Ho! I am being molested by one of my elves."

Drake laughing hysterically said,

"Glad you could make it. I guess you took the bribe to come tonight."

Jeremy raising his eyebrows responded,

"Yes. I could use the extra $600.00 to pay for extra things this year."

Sarcastically Drake responded,

"I know. Mr. Reed is attempting to appease the peasants by throwing us scraps as he plans his winter vacation in The Bahamas on his yacht. Aren't you going to introduce me to your date?"

"Sure. Drake, this is Ms. Anne. Ms. Anne, this is my friend Drake."

Ms. Anne caught Drake by surprise when she gave him a and strong and sturdy handshake and quietly said hello. He responded,

"Nice to meet you Ms. Anne. Nice handshake. There's nothing sexier that a beautiful woman with a nice strong hand shake."

Ms. Anne replied,

"Nice to meet you as well. Thank you."

Drake pointed to the stage as he said,

"There's where all the festivities will be held tonight. It should be interesting to see how things turn out."

Jeremy asked,
"Did you get a chance to talk to your mom about her back?"

Drake replied,
"I sure did. She's feeling fine and hopes we have a good time at the party tonight."

Jeremy laughed.

Drake leaned in towards Jeremy's left ear and whispered,

"It looks like your bonus is going to pay for your date tonight. How much did she cost you?"

Jeremy chucked as he said under his breath,

"She wasn't cheap. That's for sure. Look out. Here comes the life of the party."

From the corner of his eye Drake sees Mr. Reed approaching the bar. As he arrives he puts his hand on the bar and says,

"Hi Frank. I'll have a Bloody Orgasm please."

Annoyed Drake responded,

"My name is Drake, not Frank and I don't jump in the sack with the first CEO I meet."

Momentarily stunned Mr. Reed stared at Drake in silence before breaking out in a loud and contrived unrestrained laugh. Patting Drake on the shoulder he said,

"Sorry Drake, I am not so good with names. Now how about that bloody orgasm."

"Sure thing Mr. Reed. One Bloody Orgasm coming right up."

Starting to make the drink, Drake squatted to open the door to the small refrigerator under the bar and pulled out a bottle of cranberry juice and a jar of pineapple slices. Also, grabbing the glass that he had placed inside the refrigerator specifically for Mr. Reed. It contained a two ground up valium. After Standing up he placed the glass on the bar and poured the cranberry juice into the glass. He turned and grabbed a bottle of Grey Goose Vodka from the back shelf and made a long pour into the glass. After placing a slice of pineapple onto the edge of the glass he handed the drink to Mr. Reed.

"Here's your Bloody Orgasm Mr. Reed."

Mr. Reed, who had been standing with his back to the bar ogling several of the younger ladies in the room quickly turned around and snapped,

"No, it's Mr. Reed. It's not Mr. Reed. How long have you worked here son?"

Drake chuckled as he replied,

"Long enough for you to know my name. Sorry. I am not so good with names either."

Without a response, Mr. Reed took the drink from Drake and walked away."

In anticipation of him taking the first sip of his Bloody Orgasm, Drake watched Mr. Reed walk through the growing crowd of employees toward the stage. He disappeared into the ever-growing crowd of festive employees. Drake grinned as he knelt down to returned the bottle of cranberry juice to the refrigerator beneath the bar.

The room was lined with forty round dining tables that seated five. Each covered with a white linen table cloth and evenly spaced throughout the hall. A flourishing poinsettia stood as center piece.

It was a quarter till six Most of the banks employees had arrived and were seated at their assigned seats. Many were still mulling about talking to on another while others had crowded around the bar to take advantage of the free drinks. Several ladies started dancing together as the band began a rousing version of Chuck Berry's, Run Run Rudolph.

Jeremy and Ms. Anne found their way the front of the room where their table was located. After they were seated Jeremy asked Ms. Anne,

"What would you like to drink. I am headed over to the bar."

Ms. Anne smiled as she replied,

"You know. I have a taste for a Whiskey Sour."

Jeremy gently placed his hand on her shoulder as he replied,

"One Whiskey Sour coming up."

As Jeremy approached the bar he saw Drake surrounded by a loud and obnoxious group of employees who had already had one too many drinks. They appeared to Jeremy as a frenzied group of piranhas engulfing their prey. He squeezed his way through the crowd and yelled to get Drakes attention,

"Hey Drake. I'll have a Whiskey Sour and a Rum and Coke."

Drake walked over to Jeremy and said,

"Sure thing."

As Drake started preparing the two drinks he continued,

"Mr. Reed came over to the bar to get himself a drink. The douchebag didn't even know my name. Got him his drink. So, we just need to sit back and watch the show."

Jeremy looking nervously around the room to make sure no one was listening replied,

"This should be good. I haven't seen him in a few minutes, have you?"

"Not until just this very moment. Look. He's on stage. It looks like he's about to make an announcement."

Jeremy spun around to look towards the stage.
The band was about to start another song as Mr. Reed stepped up on the stage. He staggered as he approached the lead singer and asked her to step aside to make an announcement. A look of astonishment came over her face as he

131

abruptly bumped her out of the way almost knocking her over. He grabbed the microphone from the stand. Many attendees covered their ears in pain as ear splitting feedback echoed throughout the room. Mr. Reed began to speak.

Desperately attempting to maintain his balance he braced himself by clinging to the microphone stand with his free arm. It was confirmed that valium laced cocktail was taking effect. His body swayed and his eye lids drooped as he loudly chanted in a dull booming baritone voice,

"Testing, testing, testicles. Testicles! Is this thing on? Sure, it is because I can hear me. Can you hear me? "

He then closed his eyes and giggled hysterically. Many employees had turned their attention to the stage to hear what he had to say while others were still not paying attention.

The warm glow of revenge grew within Jeremy and Drake as they stood in amused silence. With mouths agape mesmerized as they watched the deeply inebriated Mr. Reed stammer and stagger on stage. Like driving past a car wreck, they couldn't look away.

Feeling ignored by the attendees of the party, Mr. Reed's caught his balance as he fell backward, cleared his throat and bellowed,

"Hey! All you happy peasants. My minions. Shut the fuck up and sit down. I am making a god damn announcement. Is that asking too much? If you don't shut the fuck up and listen no one is going to get their bonus. I am what stands between you and this month's rent payment."

His voice echoed off the walls grabbing the attention of the remaining employees. A profound silence veiled the room as the remaining employees who had been ignoring him turned their attention toward the stage. In horror, they saw their CEO stagger to the front edge of the stage in what appeared to be a deep state of inebriation and almost fall to the floor below. After regaining his balance, he stepped back and wiped away a thin line of drool from his mouth and exclaimed,

"Thank you everybody. I will be brief. Let's hear it for our bartender Drake. God damn does he make a mean Bloody Orgasm or what? I am so fucking wasted. He's the man, isn't he? Have any of you ever had a Bloody Orgasm? I just had one and wow!"

As if on cue, From the kitchen doors to the right of the stage a line of banquette staff members entered the room as they rolled out the appetizers on large metal carts. Appearing from the kitchen like a line of worker ants dressed in white dress shirts, red bow ties and black trousers, they began their march to each patrons table. The plates rattled against the metal carts making a clattering sound that enraged Mr. Reed.

With his right hand, he reached into the left side of his suit jacket and quickly withdrew a nickel-plated Smith and Wesson .357 from a shoulder holster. Women screamed and patrons ran as soon as he brandished his weapon. Many ducked for cover under their tables. Raising the gun above his head he fired off one shot into the ceiling. The boom from the gun sent the remaining diners running for the exits.

He screamed into the microphone,
"Stop! Stop with the appetizers. No one gets to eat until I am done with my announcement."
Many of the banquette staff sprinted for the exits. Several jumped under tables. Others cowered behind their food cart.

Drake and Jeremy quickly disappeared behind the bar. Jeremy's voice trembled as he said,

"Oh, my God. He's a bad drunk. I think he's going to kill someone."

Drake laughed nervously as he replied,

"God damn. He's crazier than we thought. I'll call 911."

Drake pulled out his cell phone and quickly dialed 911. As Drake spoke the emergency dispatcher there was a commotion at the entrance of the banquette room. A man was yelling at and commanding the attendees,

"Get out! Get out now. Come on people, run! Get to your cars! Move!"

Concealing himself on the other side of the door jamb to the entrance to the banquet room, Captain Tarmelli had unholstered his Glock 17. He leaned towards the entry and yelled towards Mr. Reed on the stage,

"This is Captain David Tarmelli of the Akron Police department. Put down your weapon and come out."

Mr. Reed, standing alone at the center of the stage, shaded his eyes from blinding light of the white-hot spot light looked towards the back of the room and yelled into the microphone,

"Put down my gun? You're fucking kidding me, right? Who are you? Police officer?"

Pointing his gun in the direction of Tarmelli's voice, he dropped the microphone onto the stage creating a loud thud. Staggering to his right he exited the stage down a small flight of steps. He yelled,
"Do you know who I am officer Tarmelli?"

Tarmelli remaining hidden behind the frame of the door replied,

"No. I have no idea who you are. I am not here for you. I am here for Jeremy. Jeremy Gant. Do you know him?"

Mr. Reed staggered towards Tarmelli still aiming his .357 in Taremelli's direction. He replied,

"Jeremy Gant? Crap. The name sounds familiar. Who is he?"

As Jeremy crouched behind the bar he said to Drake,

"Dude. I better go out there. Maybe I can put a stop to this before someone gets hurt."

Drake grabbed Jeremy by the arm and said,

"No fucking way. You're going to get yourself killed. There's no reason for that cop to be here for you. You haven't done anything wrong."
Before Jeremy could respond Jeremy pulled his arm from Drakes grasp jumped up from behind the bar and ran into the center of the room between Tarmelli and Mr. Reed and yelled,

"Detective! Don't shoot. Mr. Reed is just a little drunk. It's my fault. My friend and I put a valium in his drink. Apparently, he doesn't hold his liquor to well."

Mr. Reed quickly turned towards Jeremy and took aim. Leaning against one of the dining tables he wiped perspiration from his brow and said,

"Oh! Your Jeremy Gant. The guy from our call center who went to the psych ward."

Mocking Jeremy in a tiny, babies voice he said,

"Jeremy couldn't handle the pressure of a call center. Poor Jeremy is a little teeny baby who just couldn't take it."

Captain Tarmelli slowly entered the room. Calmly he said,

"Jeremy, don't get involved in this son. Get out of here before you or anyone else gets hurt. There are other officers outside that can take care of why we came here. Mr. Reed, put down your weapon and we can all go home."

Jeremy slowly walked towards Mr. Reed who had now seated himself at the table he had been leaning against. As Jeremy approached Mr. Reed stammered,

"Jeremy, are you sure you want to be a hero tonight? After all the fine captain knows what you have done. He knows all the people you have murdered. Don't you captain?"

Still keeping his weapon sighted on Mr. Reed Tarmelli asked quizzically,

"Mr. Reed, what murders are you talking about?"

Mr. Reed's eyes momentarily drooped shut. Slowly opening his eyes, he stood up and walked towards Jeremy. Stammering as he responded,

"I know you were snooping around at our call center the other day asking questions about Jeremy. His supervisor Christine told me everything. You asked about his schedule at work. You came back and went through his desk. I know everything."

Tarmelli moved to his right as he said,

"Don't move Mr. Reed. Drop your weapon right now."

Mr. Reed and Jeremy were now several feet from one another. With his gun trained on Jeremy he smiled, took a step and then awkwardly lurched towards him. Tarmelli fired his weapon striking Mr. Reed's right shoulder. Mr. Reed fell backward. His Smith and Wesson fell to the ground and slid across the carpet. Landing in-between Jeremy and the captain. Tarmelli yelled,

"Get over here Jeremy. Mr. Reed stay down! Roll onto your stomach. Put your hands behind your back!"

Jeremy ran from the banquet room and into the lobby. Drake then jumped up from behind the bar and pleaded,

"Don't shoot! I am just the bartender!"

Tarmelli responded,

"Get the hell out of here."

Drake ran from the behind the bar and into the lobby of the hall.

Sergeant Wickland burst into the room with her weapon pointed at Mr. Reed laying on the floor. She yelled,
"Don't move! Hands behind your back!"

Searing pain from his fractured shoulder made Mr. Reed cry in agony as he complied with Sergeant Wickland. She rolled him onto his back cuffing his arms behind him. After Wickland read him his Miranda rights she reached down and assisted him into a sitting position. As she searched him she asked"

"Mr. Reed, do you have any other weapons on you?"

Head bowed and fading in and out of consciousness he mumbled,

No, officer. Just my wallet and some business cards."

As Officer Wickland reached inside his coat. From his inside right lapel pocket of his suit coat she pulled a black leather wallet and a stack of plain white business cards. The cards were partially saturated with his own blood. Printed on one side of each of the cards the inscription read,
"Press One for Murder."

19 EPILOGUE

Di Nardo Party Center was now encircled by scores of police cars, a fire engine and an ambulance. The stucco sided facility was bathed in the red and blue strobes of the police cruisers and emergency vehicles. Many of the partygoers jumped into their cars after escaping the ball room and fled to their homes. The remaining employees of the bank were scattered throughout the parking lot and the lobby of the building. Some were being interviewed by police officers to get their take on what had just happened. Others stood in shock, shivering in the cold, waiting to give their eye witness account.

The paramedics had made their way into the party center to provide aid to Mr. Reed. Strapped down to a hospital gurney with his blood-soaked shirt cut open, the paramedics attended to his wounded shoulder. Captain Tarmelli stood to the side questioning Mr. Reed.

"Mr. Reed, do you know where you are?"

Gasping for breath from behind an oxygen mask Mr. Reed replied,

"Yes, I am at my companies Christmas party at the Di Nardo Party Center."

"Do you know why we came here tonight?"

"No idea."

"We went back to your offices to take a look through the desk of one of your employees. We suspect him of.."

"Before Tarmelli could finish Mr. Reed interrupted,

"Murder. You suspected Jeremy Gant of being a serial murderer."

Looking surprised Tarmelli responded,

"Yes. That's correct. How did you know?"

Mr. Reed winced in pain as the paramedics applied pressure to his wound with a padded gauze bandage to help stop the bleeding. He gritted his teeth as he replied,

"The first time you came to our call center to speak to Jeremy, our guard, Brandon, called me in my office to let me know you were there. He wasn't sure why you were there but said you were speaking to Jeremy and his supervisor Christine. After you left, Christine, called me to let me know that you spoke to her. She said that you suspected Jeremy as a possible suspect in a series of murders in the Akron area and that you asked her to give you a call if you saw anything unusual from Jeremy."

The paramedic interrupted,

"Chief, we have him patched up. His wound is a through and through but we've got to get him into the E.R. He's lost a lot of blood."

Tarmelli nodded his head in agreement and said,

"Just another minute and he's all yours."

Turning his attention back to Mr. Reed he asked,

"Did you put the business cards under his keyboard?"

"Yes. When I heard that you guys thought he was the suspect I couldn't have been more amused. Jeremy's one of our best employees. I thought it was the perfect opportunity to divert any attention from me to him. So, after everyone went home for the night, I stayed behind and slipped the cards under his keyboard."

Tarmelli asked,

"So, tell me. How did you choose the people you killed?"

Mr. Reed coughed and then responded,

"Any time one of our customers threatened any of our call center representatives or made a direct threat to the call center facility, each customer service representative is required to fill out a report and give it to our guard, Brandon. Brandon in turn calls the police. He also gives me a copy of the report. I would often follow up with some of the customers on the report by calling them on the phone to try and smooth things out with them. You know, I thought as the CEO of Midland giving them a call to offer my apologies and to see how I could make things right would in and of itself make them believe I cared. But many of these people were disgusting ungrateful individuals. White trash slobs mostly. They threatened me no matter what I said or how generous my offers were to make things right."

Mr. Reeds voice trailed off and his eyes rolled back into his head as he began to pass out. The loss of blood combined with the tranquilizers were having serious effects on him.

Tarmelli said loudly,

"Mr. Reed! Wake up! Wake up"

Mr. Reeds eyes opened slowly. He lifted his head from the pillow and with his speech slurred he responded,

"I made a list, I checked it twice, saw who was naughty and who was nice and killed me some white trash people. Trust me the world is a better place without them."

Mr. Reed's head fell back, he closed his eyes and drifted into unconsciousness. The effects of the wound combined with the tranquilizer drifting through his mind had begun to take their toll.

The paramedic said with urgency,

"He's in bad shape. We've got to get him transported to the emergency room fast!"

Tarmelli replied,

"Ok. Keep him alive. We've got to find out if there are victims we don't know about."

The paramedics rushed Mr. Reed from the lobby and quickly loaded him into the ambulance. With sirens blaring they drove into the cold December night.

Tarmelli walked over to Jeremy who was being detained by an officer at the front of the lobby and said,

"Mr. Gant. I owe you a huge apology. Officer, take your cuffs off of Mr. Gant. He is free to go."

After the hand cuffs were removed from Jeremy, Tarmelli reached out and shook Jeremy's hand.

They shook hands and Jeremy responded,

"I am not sure what to say. Mr. Reed was a living breathing, walking prick but I would have never guessed he was a serial killer."

Tarmelli raised his eyebrows and said,

"You never can tell. You never can tell."

About the author

Peter Tompkins was born in autumn of 1965 in Cleveland, Ohio and grew up in Chardon, Ohio where he attended Chardon High School. After graduating high school, he attended Ohio University to study Graphic Design and Business Management.

Upon getting his Bachelors in Fine Art and Business Management he spent a short time working in Corporate America as a Telecommunications Support Technician and Call Center Representative. In late 2007, he decided to quit the rate race start his own business. Skating Bear Studios was born. There he integrated his eye for composition, design and photography to create stunning visual compositions.

Peter is also a singer/songwriter and author of over one hundred and fifty original compositions. As an avid Beatles fan he was inspired to learn to play guitar and write songs. He got his first guitar at the age of fifteen and has been performing as a solo acoustic performer in front of audiences since his early 20's.

His writings incorporate his love for the rock group The Beatles, his time working in a call center and his upbringing in northeast Ohio.

Made in the USA
Middletown, DE
01 September 2023

37806211R00090